The pain ... ... a dull throb.
She ought to be deciding what she was going to do
next, making new plans. She realized that she hadn't
thought things out in detail, not beyond reaching this
place where she could rest and heal. And now even
that plan had been destroyed by the presence of the
unexpected stranger downstairs.

Not that the stranger hadn't behaved admirably,
once he got over his first impression that she was a
burglar, Karen admitted to herself. He had been very
helpful, very kind. Almost too kind. She was aware
that he had acted with exactly the sort of solicitude
that he would have shown to any young woman. She
shouldn't confuse politeness with interest.

On the other hand, that little moment of breathlessness
had not been the product of her imagination. She
wriggled down into the coziness of the quilts as
she savored it again. It had been a long time since
she had felt anything like that. Perhaps ... from
now on ... there would be other such moments in
her life. . . .

Dear Reader,

Though it may be cold outside during the month of November, it's always warmed by the promise of the upcoming holiday season. What better time to curl up with a good book? What better time for Silhouette Romance?

And in November, we've got some wonderful books to take the chill off these cold winter months. Continuing our DIAMOND JUBILEE celebration is *Song of the Lorelei*, by Lucy Gordon. Escape to the romantic world of brooding Conrad von Feldstein. The haunting secret at von Feldstein Castle is revealed when beautiful Laurel Blake pays a visit... and love finally comes home. Don't miss this emotional, poignant tale!

The DIAMOND JUBILEE—Silhouette Romance's tenth anniversary celebration—is our way of saying thanks to you, our readers. To symbolize the timelessness of love, as well as the modern gift of the tenth anniversary, we're presenting readers with a DIAMOND JUBILEE Silhouette Romance each month, penned by one of your favorite Silhouette Romance authors. And rounding up the year, next month be sure to watch for *Only the Nanny Knows for Sure*, by Phyllis Halldorson.

And that's not all! There are six books a month from Silhouette Romance—stories by wonderful writers who, time and time again, bring home the magic of love. During our anniversary year, each book is special and written with romance in mind. This month, and in the future, work by such loved writers as Diana Palmer, Brittany Young and Annette Broadrick is sure to put a smile on your face.

During our tenth anniversary, the spirit of celebration is with us year-round. And that's all due to you, our readers. With the support you've given to us, you can look forward to many more years of heartwarming, poignant love stories.

I hope you'll enjoy this book and all of the stories to come. Come home to romance—Silhouette Romance—for always!

Sincerely,
Tara Hughes Gavin
Senior Editor

WYNN WILLIAMS

One Breathless Moment

Silhouette Romance

Published by Silhouette Books New York

America's Publisher of Contemporary Romance

SILHOUETTE BOOKS
300 E. 42nd St., New York, N.Y. 10017

ISBN: 0-373-08756-X

First Silhouette Books printing November 1990

Printed in the U.S.A.

Books by Wynn Williams

Silhouette Romance

Starry Nights #649
One Breathless Moment #756

Silhouette Special Edition

*White Nights #417

*coauthored as Dee Norman

WYNN WILLIAMS

was born in Canada but has lived in the Pacific Northwest for most of her life. Her dream was to be an author, and now she travels with her engineer husband to research new locations for her romance novels.

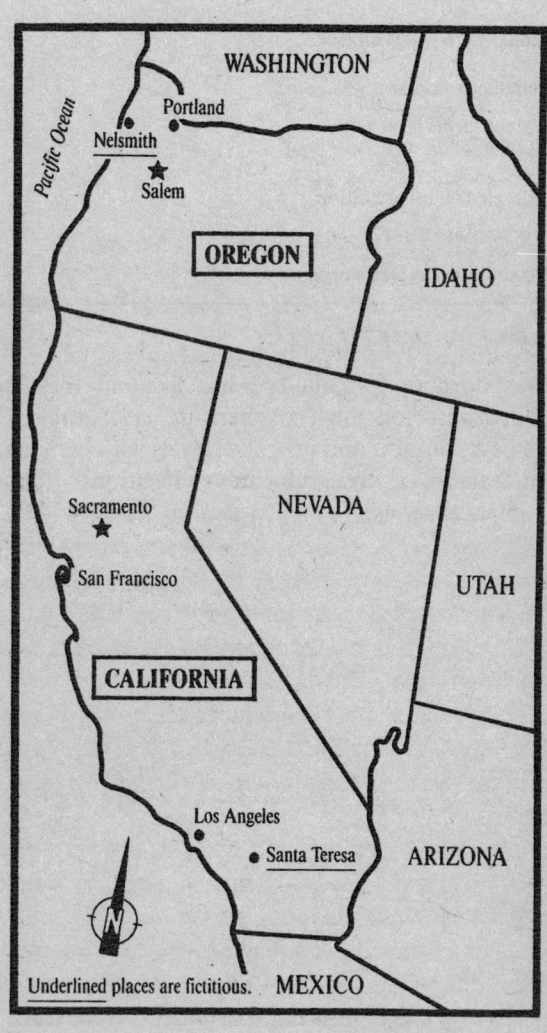

WASHINGTON

Pacific Ocean

Portland
Nelsmith
★
Salem

OREGON

IDAHO

Sacramento
★

San Francisco

NEVADA

UTAH

CALIFORNIA

Los Angeles
● Santa Teresa

ARIZONA

N

Underlined places are fictitious. MEXICO

Chapter One

Rain slashed against the windows of the small Beach bus as it bored northward into the night. Karen Grenville leaned her face close to the window and cupped her hands around her eyes, searching for recognizable landmarks along the road. The darkness outside turned each rectangle of glass into a black mirror that reflected the dimly lit interior of the vehicle and its handful of passengers. Roadside lights were infrequent along this part of the coast highway; the Pacific Ocean remained only a great unseen presence completely obscured by the fury of the storm.

The isolation of the long bus journey up from Santa Teresa had served to dull Karen's anxieties. But she had hoped to find a welcoming peace, a healing tranquility, once her destination was reached. Now the lateness of the hour and the black fury of the storm promised only further misery and confusion. The closer the bus came to the little coastal town of Nelsmith, the stronger Karen's reluctance became.

She couldn't possibly face her aunt Minna's stern countenance in her present exhausted condition. It was bad enough to arrive without warning, but to show up in the middle of the night, soaked to the skin—Karen shivered at the thought. Thank goodness there was an alternative...if she could persuade the bus driver to cooperate.

She finally spied what she was looking for; a crossroad with a single streetlight that illuminated a handful of weathered buildings standing dark and silent in the rain. Now she knew where she was. Karen picked up her purse and light suitcase and gathered her padded jacket around her. Her heart beat hard as she made her way toward the front of the bus.

She stopped at the driver's shoulder and spoke in low, guarded tones. "Would you please stop and let me off at the next crossroad?" she asked, her voice quavering with nervousness.

"I couldn't do that. Not in this kind of weather. And this time of night." He spoke without looking at her. "Nelsmith is just another few miles up the road."

There it was, the flat refusal she had feared. She took a deep breath. "Please! It's important to me."

When he did not respond, Karen moved forward a little, into the glow of light from the dashboard. She looked at him pleadingly. His eyes widened slightly, and she knew he had noticed the yellowing bruise high on her left cheek, the fresher one on the point of her jaw, the cut on her forehead....

"I—I really don't want to go into Nelsmith," she said with a catch in her voice that was perfectly genuine. "Everything will be closed and dark."

His expression softened. But he shook his head. "I can't just put you off in the middle of nowhere like this. You'd get soaked."

"My house is right there, right by the road," she said swiftly. "In two minutes I'll be dry and safe inside." More than safety, what she needed was a hideaway, a haven in a painful and frustrating world.

"Well..." he said, obviously still uneasy with the idea. He looked at her searchingly again. The bus began to slow down.

"Oh, thank you!" she said. She stood by the door and zipped her jacket shut and tied a scarf beneath her chin while he braked to a careful halt so smoothly that few of the sleeping passengers would even be aware of the stop. Karen stepped down onto the black shoulder of the road and turned to face the storm.

She staggered as the fierce wind buffeted her in the darkness, and the persistent dull pain in her head jolted into momentary agony. The gale from the west drove sheets of rain before it. Cold wetness filled the air. Her hip-length jacket partially protected her, but her jeans and tennis shoes became immediately sodden. Her scarf and hair were streaming with water by the time she found the rutted dirt road that led from the highway to the beach.

She put her head down and felt her way gingerly in the darkness. Two minutes to the house, she had told the bus driver, because otherwise he would never have been persuaded to let her out. But it was farther than that. On a bright summer day she might walk it in five minutes. On a wild pitch-black night like this one, she'd be lucky to stumble her way to the front door in a quarter of an hour.

She could feel her jacket growing heavier, dragging on her shoulders as the rain penetrated the outer shell, soaking into the padding. The October chill seemed to work its way into her very bones as she trudged along. At last she sensed the nearness of the house, feeling it before she could see it, a blacker bulk looming up in the darkness.

She stepped up onto the porch and groped blindly along the edge of the door frame, searching for the key in its familiar hiding place. Her wet fingers, numb with cold, failed to recognize the little niche the first time they touched it. She felt a moment of panic, then relief washed over her as she found the key just where it was supposed to be, where it was always kept for the convenience of the family.

The gale blew the door open as she turned the knob, blew her stumbling inside, made a stir and a rustling all around the dark interior of the room before she could slam the door firmly and reach for the light switch.

She saw a blizzard of white paper strewn around the big comfortable living room. Pages covered with numbers lay scattered over the blue rug and on the chintz-covered couch. They fluttered from the old maple rocker and the wide brick hearth.

"What the hell are you doing in my house!" A tall tousle-haired figure in dark red pajama trousers filled the bedroom doorway, filled the room with sudden menace.

Karen looked around her, panicky, trapped. "This *isn't* your house! It can't be. It's my aunt's house. Minna would have let me know if she'd sold it."

His doubled fists relaxed into large capable masculine hands. His stance became slightly less threatening, although the straight black brows still drew together in a forbidding frown. "Evidently she didn't feel she was required to notify you whenever she rented her property."

"Rented! You mean you're living here? For how long?" she demanded, too dismayed to care how ungracious her words sounded.

"I've been here eight days, if it's any of your business. And I intend to stay until my project is finished." He glanced meaningfully at the papers scattered around the room. "Which may take longer than I had expected."

"I'm sorry," Karen said belatedly. Her mind had been so fastened on the idea of this house as a hideaway that the change in the situation made her feel numb, disoriented.

"Apology accepted, though it hardly remedies the situation," he said shortly. "Now, why don't you get back in your car and go blow somebody else's work all to pieces."

"I didn't come in a car." Karen groped for the doorknob, exhaustion sweeping over her. She steadied herself against the door. "I walked down from the highway." Water was running off her clothes, darkening the rug around her feet.

He saw her face go white. His mind sharpened as he shook off the disorienting effect of being yanked out of a sound sleep to face a midnight intruder.

"You look like a drowned cat," he said with a touch of concern in his voice. He took a step toward her, and she shrank back.

He stopped, perplexed. He spread his hands and tried to look harmless. "Let's start over again," he said quietly. "I'm Jeff Forrester, and it happens that I've rented this place for an indefinite period of time—however long it takes me to finish this job I'm working on. You know what I mean—peace and quiet and no interruptions. I apologize for yelling at you. Why don't you come in and sit down and let me turn up the heat and find you a towel?"

She nodded wordlessly. Jeff held out his hand. After a pause she unzipped the soaking jacket and let him take it from her. He gathered up the papers that had landed around the wooden rocker by the hearth. She came forward, trailing drops of water behind her, to settle into it.

Jeff hung the jacket on the shower head in the bathroom and took a couple of big white towels from the shelf. He detoured into his bedroom to pick up his warm woolen bathrobe.

"Why don't you take off your wet things and put this on?" he asked with gentle persuasion. "I'll go out in the kitchen and make us some coffee."

As the coffee maker began its cycle, he could hear her moving around softly in the living room. He took the opportunity to duck back into the bedroom and pull on a sweatshirt, jeans and a pair of well-worn running shoes.

When he carried in the two cups of steaming coffee, she was sitting in the rocker with her feet tucked under her, wrapped in the voluminous folds of his robe.

"I put milk and sugar in yours," he said. "You look like you need it." He noticed that she clasped both hands around the cup for its heat. "And let me bring you some warm socks to put on."

She accepted his wooliest socks with whispered thanks. He couldn't help noticing as she put them on that one slender tanned leg bore an ugly purple bruise. Looking for further ways to reassure her, he started to build a fire in the fireplace on the ashes of the last one, not so much for the warmth it could add to the room, but for the calming influence of the softly crackling flames.

As he sat on the hearth, stoking the fire, he thought that the drowned cat comparison had been an appropriate one. He had never seen anyone who looked quite so forlorn. He eyed her covertly, thinking that the triangular little face and the green eyes reinforced the feline image. The thick shoulder-length brown hair, toweled and combed now, hung straight down on either side of her face, half hiding her features when she looked down at her hands broodingly, as she was doing now. Her mouth was wide and generous, but all the lipstick had been bitten off the full lower lip. Her nose was very slightly crooked. With those marks on her face—the bruises, the cut—she looked wounded and vulnerable. A very bedraggled little lost kitten had come to his door to find shelter from the rain.

Curiosity burned inside of him, to his surprise. What had happened to his usual detachment? It wasn't like him to get involved in a stranger's business, whatever it was. He wanted to know her story, but instinct told him that he had to take it slowly, had to let her get used to him. He stirred and she looked up with a start.

"I'm sorry," she said again, as though she was accustomed to apologizing her way through life.

Jeff wondered what—or who—had done this to her. There were no rings on her fingers, so perhaps it was not an abusive husband who had bruised her body and undermined her spirit.

"Don't be sorry," he assured her. "Now that I'm fully awake and aware that you are not a burglar, this is a rather stimulating break in the humdrum pattern of my days."

"You don't look like a man who is hungry for breaks in his routine," she said with an insight that surprised him.

"What kind of a man *do* I look like, then?" He was half teasing, half intrigued.

"I think you're a man who loves his work," she said shyly. "I'm sorry for the interruption. And the mess."

"It's fair to say that the wind made the mess, not you. And I must admit that this seems like a rather more interesting interruption than most of them." She closed her eyes and leaned back in the chair. He looked at her sharply. "When did you eat last?"

"Before I got on the bus, I guess," she said vaguely. "I wasn't hungry."

Jeff thought that she looked ready to drop. Perhaps if he could get some food into her, some more sugar... He got to his feet. "I'll make us some toast," he said too positively for any denial.

He brought her two slices of buttered toast on a dinner plate and a pint jar of jam with a spoon standing up in it. She accepted the clumsy offering politely, broke one piece of toast in two and spread a small spoonful of the dark red jam on it. He was unprepared for the fleeting smile that suddenly illuminated her face.

"Aunt Minna's marionberry jam!" she said. "It's not the best in the world, but we always say that it's the most distinctive."

He folded himself down to sit on the low hearth again. "That's right. When she brought it around a few days ago, she told me that it has a secret ingredient. I can't figure out what it is, but I'm beginning to acquire a taste for it."

"Would you like some of this?" Karen asked as though belatedly remembering her manners.

"Good idea," Jeff said. "Just put some jam on that other piece for me, will you?" She seemed to be more sure of herself as she performed this small domestic task, and he silently congratulated himself that he was using the right psychology to win her confidence. "I'll make some more when this is gone," he went on. "I'm not much good in a kitchen, but I know my way around a toaster."

She ate almost greedily, and he replenished the plate twice before she sat back with a little sigh of repletion. He leaned forward to refill her cup from the coffeepot he had brought in from the kitchen. "Would you like to tell me what the trouble is?" he asked matter-of factly.

Her hands came up to touch her face, over her bruises. After a pause she said, "I was in a car accident." But the statement sounded almost like a question, as though she was asking him if he would accept that explanation.

Perplexed, he decided to try a more oblique approach. "I don't even know your name," he said.

"I'm sorry." Her hands dropped to her lap again. "I'm Karen Grenville. Minna is my aunt, my father's sister. My father's an engineer. He's out of the country most of the time. Right now he's in the Philippines. This house has been in the family as long as I can remember. I knew that Minna had finally moved into town and started to rent the old place during the summer, but I never expected anyone to be staying here this time of year. That's why I barged in on you like this."

Jeff regarded her thoughtfully. None of the pieces of this puzzle seemed to fit. "But where did you come from? And how did you get here—in the middle of the night and without a car?"

"I came from—from California," she said vaguely. "By bus. I asked the driver to let me off on the highway, and I walked down the road."

She didn't look as if she was lying, Jeff thought. But surely it would have made more sense to ride all the way into town and contact her aunt from there. Especially at this time of night and in this kind of weather.

She stared at him almost defiantly. "I didn't know that the bus was going to be late." Her voice was defensive. "All this rain caused a mud slide on the highway south of here. The road was blocked on the other side of Tilla-mook. We waited for hours before we could get through. Everything in Nelsmith will be closed up tight by now."

She absentmindedly touched her fingertips to a bruise on her cheek where the ugly color was just beginning to fade at the edges. "I haven't been up to visit since Minna moved into her new house. I'm not even certain just where it is. It seemed simpler to come straight here."

Jeff got to his feet and walked around the room, picking up a few of the scattered papers from the furniture, using the activity as an excuse to hide the skepticism he could feel written plainly on his face.

Did it make good sense for her to come to an empty house, one that was dark and cold, with no food in the kitchen, rather than go to the family warmth of her aunt's place? There must be more to the situation than she was telling him.

"Perhaps you should call your aunt," he suggested. "She'll be worried since you haven't shown up."

Karen stared into the fire as though to avoid his eyes. "Minna's not expecting me," she said finally. "I didn't let her know I was coming."

He frowned. "You didn't tell her? Were you planning to knock on the door and say 'Surprise'? Shouldn't you have invested in a thirty-second telephone call just in case she wasn't home?"

Karen read disapproval in the tightening of his lips, the altered tone of his voice. "All I wanted was to come here and be by myself with nobody nagging me and bossing me around!" she burst out. "Just a little peace and quiet until these bruises fade away, and—and my nerves calm down a little, enough that I can go back to work."

"And who's been nagging you and bossing you around?" Jeff sounded less friendly than before.

"Edward. My ex-husband. He insists that everything that's happened to me just proves that I can't make it on my own. That I was wrong to ever leave him." Her listener's dubious expression remained the same. She felt a spark of anger, a little stirring of vitality deep inside of her.

"I *would* have telephoned Minna, but that meant one other person telling me that I need Edward to take care of me. And she'd tell him where I was. I was afraid that as soon as I stepped in her front door, there'd be a call from him, explaining that running away like this is just a—a further demonstration of my fundamental inadequacy. He'd order me to stop being childish and come home where I belong." She pushed her hair back from her face. "Edward might even come all the way up here so he could badger me some more. Just like he did in the hospital."

"You were in the hospital?" Jeff looked down at her.

"Not for long. I had bruises, scrapes, shock. And a mild concussion. The pain in my head wasn't mild, though. I did try to go right back to work, but I couldn't manage it." She looked up. "It was my boss's idea to take a few days off, to get some rest and quiet...." She let her voice trail away.

"So you come here and step off a bus straight into the worst storm of the year," Jeff supplied.

"I don't care about the weather. I *love* a storm—as long as I'm inside and dry."

"I feel the same way," he said. "I'm beginning to understand—at least I think I am."

"I've been telling it all backward, starting at the end instead of the beginning." She closed her eyes and rested her head against the wooden back of the rocking chair. "It began a week ago, when I had my purse snatched outside my apartment. I grabbed on to the strap, so the man hit me, punched me in the face to make me let go."

"You say 'I had my purse snatched' as though you were responsible. As though you made it happen."

She gave him a level look. "Edward brought me roses and pointed out that I had used my customary poor judgment by hanging on and making it necessary for the man to hit me. And by living in a neighborhood where such things can happen. Two more reasons that I ought to come back to him where I belong." She let her eyelids drift shut again. "Well, I had this big bruise on my cheek, and all my credit cards had to be replaced. And when I went to get a new driver's license, this accident happened while I was driving home. The driver behind me ran a stoplight. That totaled my car and put me in the hospital for two days. And when I got out, I was too shaky to do my job properly. So here I am."

Reluctantly she began to uncurl from her comfortable position. "And now I'd better make that call to Minna and go through the whole story again."

"It's late," said Jeff. "Nearly two in the morning."

"I've imposed on your hospitality enough for one night." Karen stood up and slowly turned toward the telephone, feeling her resolve diminish. Explaining all this to Minna, making her understand, seemed almost too great an effort to undertake.

Jeff said, "You could spend the night here. And call her in the morning when you're rested."

"Oh, no, I couldn't do that." The words came to her lips without conscious thought on her part.

"It's a big house. I'm not using any of the upstairs rooms."

"I couldn't," she repeated. "Thank you—that's very generous. But I couldn't."

He gave an almost imperceptible shrug. A fleeting expression—impatience? annoyance? scorn?—crossed his rugged features before he controlled it, changing it to polite indifference.

That sudden withdrawal stabbed her unexpectedly. This past hour, this little haven of warm friendliness, was too precious to be hastily destroyed. "I'm sorry. It's just that—that my aunt would never understand."

He looked at her, quite expressionless now. "It doesn't sound so difficult to me. You're exhausted. The storm is at its height. And you're hardly up to another cross-examination in the middle of the night."

"Yes, but—" Karen searched for the words to explain. "She *is* my aunt. She just wouldn't like it if I—if I stayed here all night."

"She sounds fairly unreasonable. And you sound like a teenager with a curfew."

And you sound like another person ready and eager to order my life, she thought, feeling a flash of rebellion. She stiffened a little. "Nelsmith is a very small place. The people here know me—I lived here with Minna for two years after my mother died. You know how small towns are. People gossip."

"Is that what you're afraid of? Who's going to tell them? And why should you care so much about what people might say?"

"Minna cares. She has to live here. She'll be very upset with me if I start her friends whispering behind her back. I just can't do it."

He frowned. "Even if it means going out in this storm again?"

She was silent for a moment, listening to the rain drumming against the side of the old house. Gusts of wind rattled the windows. She shivered. Making a great effort, she forced herself to get to her feet. All of a sudden, the warm glow of lamplight and firelight seemed too precious to turn her back upon. The storms within and without were too formidable for her shattered nerves to brave. She buried her face in her hands.

"I'm sorry," he said.

Karen couldn't believe that he was sorry at all. At least, not for anything that *he* had done or said. He was probably sorry that he had a fuzzy-minded female on his hands, someone who wouldn't be guided by his superior intelligence, who wasn't listening to his words of wisdom, who wouldn't do as he told her "for her own good." The nerve-racking misery of the past week was all at once compounded by an overwhelming fatigue that engulfed her. She started to speak, and the words turned into sobs, sobs that became deeper, and harsher, and unstoppable.

Strong hands grasped her shoulders. Head down, sobbing, shaking, she tried to twist away from him. He tightened his grasp until finally she stopped resisting, let herself relax against him. Strong arms encircled her, holding her tight. Her sobs gradually died away and her body stilled as his warmth and strength calmed her shaken nerves. She felt his heartbeat steady against her own, providing a surprising amount of comfort. They stood like that in the circle of firelight for what seemed a long period of time. Karen felt peaceful and safe as she had not felt for many days.

When she could control her voice again, she tipped her head back to look at him. "You should have slapped my face. Isn't that the approved treatment for hysterical women?"

"I can think of other things to do to that face besides slapping it," Jeff said quietly.

Karen was aware of a blush rising, burning the skin of her cheeks, but that awareness faded away into a kind of breathlessness, a moment that seemed suspended outside time....

He made no further move, said no more, as his dark eyes gazed steadily into hers. She was forced to look away as embarrassment flooded over her. What was she doing? What had she expected—passionate kisses, as though she was some femme fatale who could drive a helpless stranger wild? Not likely, not with a face like hers. She, too, could think of other things to do with her face besides slapping it.

"I know what it *needs*," she told him.

"Yes?" he said, waiting for her to go on.

She started to explain, then stopped abruptly. This stranger had been patient and kind, but he didn't want to hear her life history, to know about all her plans that had never worked out. She hadn't made them come true yet, that was all. But someday...

Chapter Two

Jeff was looking down at her, waiting for her to explain. Karen looked away in confusion. The rain lashed against the windows. The wind rattled the glass.

"It's not important," she said faintly.

"You look exhausted," he said in a soothing voice.

He's humoring me, thought Karen. But she was too tired to be indignant. She brought herself back to her present problems with an effort. The food, the fire, and someone to unburden herself to—all these comforts had made her forget that this refuge she had struggled to reach was no longer available to her. The old house shook under a fresh onslaught of the wind, and she flinched at its fury.

His gaze sharpened. "You're in no shape to go out in this. Would it really be so terrible if you stayed the rest of the night here?"

Karen thought that he sounded faintly insulted by her insistence on leaving, as though she didn't trust him.

Looking at it from his point of view, it would seem that she would rather face the fiercest storm, brave her dragon of an aunt in the dead of night—anything rather than stay under the same roof with him.

It would be so simple, so easy, to walk upstairs and lie down in her old familiar bed. To close her eyes and put off all the problems and perplexities that were crowding in on her. The thought was tempting—do what was easy and ignore for once the dictates of her family.

"Well?" said Jeff.

Karen had a mental picture of her aunt's unsmiling countenance. "It's Minna," she said.

Jeff made an impatient gesture. "You still feel you have to answer to her?"

"Well, I couldn't tell her a *lie*." He didn't know what it was like to stand up to the strong-minded members of her family. She thought of her pretty, pliant mother, always sighing and agreeing, smoothing over prickly situations, keeping the peace at the cost of her own desires. A stranger couldn't understand. Or could he? She looked at him speculatively. It was more likely that he was one of *them*. One of the forceful, always right, lets-have-no-more-argument-out-of-you people. Right now he seemed more baffled than anything else. And she could understand that. When he looked at her, he was seeing a grown woman, presumably one with a normal amount of backbone. After all, she was free and independent and nearly twenty-seven years old, no child anymore. So why couldn't she just make up her mind and do this small thing? Especially since it made better sense when one looked at it from his perspective—a good night's sleep all around, and nobody would have to go back out in the rain.

The house shook again to the force of the wind, as though reminding her of the storm outside.

Karen closed her eyes and put a hand to her throbbing head. Exhaustion won out over convention. "I'll call Minna in the morning," she said.

"Take your choice of the upstairs rooms," he said. "I'm not using any of them."

She nodded vaguely and looked around for her suitcase. She had dropped it just inside the front door. He followed her gaze and went over to pick it up before she could move toward it. He carried the small case to the stairway while she followed, a new trepidation making her heart beat faster. Had he understood that she was agreeing to a night's shelter—and nothing more?

He set the suitcase on the third step and stood aside to make way for her. "The top of the house is yours," he said tactfully. "Sleep as late as you want."

Standing alone in the upstairs hall, she felt for the first time that she had reached a safe harbor in the center of her life's storms. Force of habit turned her toward the small bedroom that had always been hers, the one that faced inland toward the first rise of the Coast Range on the far side of the highway. Then a sudden small streak of willfulness made her pause, turned her in the other direction toward the big room in front. In here, the storm battered noisily at the westward-facing windows. But the lights, warmth and solitude gave her the paradoxical feeling of being securely sheltered at last. And in the morning she would awake to a view of the sea.

Karen woke slowly from a long luxurious sleep, woke to a feeling of comfort and well-being that she had not experienced for many days. She lay snug and drowsy under the warm quilts, reluctant to leave their shelter and face the world.

The room's tall windows overlooked the ocean. The light that came in through them showed her that the storm had nearly blown itself out. Pale, watery sunshine struggled through breaks in the fast-moving gray clouds. The angle of the light suggested that the day was well along toward noon.

Karen closed her eyes again. The pain in her head had subsided to a dull throb. She ought to be deciding what she was going to do next, making new plans. She realized that she hadn't thought things out in detail, not beyond reaching this place, where she could rest and heal. And now even that plan had been destroyed by the presence of the unexpected stranger downstairs.

Not that the stranger hadn't behaved admirably, once he'd got over his first impression that she was a burglar, Karen admitted to herself. He had been very helpful, very kind. Almost too kind. She was aware that he had acted with exactly the sort of solicitude that he would have shown to any young woman whose mental equilibrium was seriously in doubt. And it didn't mean a thing last night when he said that there were better things to do with her face than slapping it. She shouldn't confuse politeness with interest.

On the other hand, that little moment of breathlessness had not been a product of her imagination. She wriggled down into the coziness of the quilts as she savored it again. It had been a long time since she had felt anything like that. Perhaps...once she had her new face...there might be other such moments in her life....

She felt herself slipping into her old daydreams of a new face, a new start, when everything would be different....

Not now, she told herself reluctantly. There were too many things she had to do before she could go back to dreaming. And she had to start by getting out of bed.

Karen belted Jeff's warm bathrobe around her slim waist and went downstairs. As she passed through the living room, the clock on the mantel showed her that it was nearly one-thirty in the afternoon. She had slept even later than she realized. The kitchen seemed untouched. The plate and cups in the sink were the ones they had used last night. There was no sign that anyone had eaten here this morning.

She looked around, puzzled, a little worried. She listened, but there was no sound in the house except for the hum of the big old refrigerator. A sudden coldness of fear swept over her. Had he gone? Was she alone? Had something happened?

Quietly she checked the rest of the downstairs rooms. Her host's bedroom door was open and the bed unmade, the sheets and blankets in a tangle. In the bathroom her blue padded jacket hung on the shower head. The door to the other downstairs bedroom was shut tight. She stopped in front of it and listened for sounds of movement inside. Nothing. Hesitantly she knocked, very lightly.

After a long pause Jeff's voice said, "Yes?"

She opened the door, just a crack at first, then wider. The largest bedroom in the house had been transformed into a workroom. A computer table and desk were covered with books and papers.

Jeff glanced up from the computer keyboard in front of him. "Oh, hi," he said absently, and went on working.

Karen remained in the doorway, ignored, until her surprise turned into annoyance, both with him and with herself. Well, she told herself, what had she been expecting, anyhow? Had she been weaving fantasies of romantic intrigue in the back of her mind? Mystery Woman Out of the Storm spends stolen night with Tall Dark Stranger? That sort of thing? And then what had she expected the morning to bring? Certainly not that Tall Dark Stranger would apparently have forgotten Mystery Woman's very existence.

Did you really think you were so memorable? said a familiar little jeering voice in the back of her head. Never mind, Karen told herself crossly. To Jeff, she said, "Did you eat any breakfast?"

"Breakfast?" he said without looking up. There was another long pause. "I don't think so."

She decided to take another tack. "Well, are you hungry?"

"Hungry?" He appeared to think about it for a moment. "Yes," he said.

"Will you stop to eat if I fix us something? Or would you rather have a sandwich in here?" It seemed the least she could do after he had given her shelter for the night.

He answered more quickly this time. "I'll stop. Give me fifteen minutes. Maybe twenty."

Karen closed the door quietly as she left, though she doubted he would have noticed if she had slammed it. She rolled up the too-long sleeves of the bathrobe on her way back to the kitchen.

These surroundings were familiar. Even before she had come to live with Minna, she had spent many summers and holidays in this house. She moved efficiently, her fragile self-confidence beginning to revive. Ordinarily she would be nervous at the mere thought of making a meal for a stranger. But this stranger—when he remembered to eat—seemed to be existing on frozen dinners and things out of cans, judging by the state of the refrigerator and the trash. She could do better than that.

He had apparently stocked up on groceries at one time, but the egg carton was still full, the bacon still tightly sealed. A head of lettuce had turned rusty, but the tomatoes felt firm. She found green onions, and some cheese only slightly dried out from being put away without a wrapper.

When she went to summon him, she entered the workroom without knocking. He was oblivious to her presence until she touched him on the shoulder. "Come and eat," she said.

"Okay," Jeff answered vaguely, continuing to work. "Fine. Right away."

She waited for a count of ten. "Or shall I bring it in here?"

He looked at her then and came at least part of the way back to the present moment. His eyes saw her instead of seeing through her. "I'll leave this right now," he said, and pushed his chair back.

His three-egg omelet, as golden brown as a magazine illustration and filled with tomatoes, onion and cheese, slid out of the pan to cover most of his plate. She dished up crisp bacon for the two of them, buttered the toast hot out of the toaster and sat down opposite him.

He ate in hungry silence. "What a meal!" he said appreciatively. "You can call me away from work for food like this anytime."

Karen shook her head with a smile. "Not just anytime, I bet. Not with your powers of concentration. You'd only be lured away at times like this—when you haven't had any breakfast or lunch, for some reason."

He leaned toward her, inner excitement lighting up his dark eyes. "I've been going up a blind alley for a week, getting nowhere. Then I woke up this morning and saw what I've been doing wrong. It was as plain as day! And I owe it all to you!"

"To me?" she said. "What did I have to do with it?"

"For days now I've been going over and over and over the same thing, night and day, like a needle stuck in a groove. Then you came along and jolted my attention completely out of its rut. Freed up my subconscious to let go and try a new approach. The right approach, this time."

His pleasure and enthusiasm brought a shadow of a smile to her lips. She could see why her aunt might have grown fond of him, fond enough to bring him her own special brand of jam. His strong, bony features were not handsome, but the dark eyes shone with intelligence and with the contagious excitement of a man who does difficult work, does it well and loves every minute of it.

"Just what are you doing that I have been such a great help at?" she asked.

He refilled his coffee cup and settled back to explain. "I'm updating my word-processing program. Working on the editor. It's almost like—like giving it a heart transplant."

"A *what*?"

He frowned, searching for the words that would make her understand. "In previous versions, the program had a file size limit. When I get through with this, it will be able to use all the available DOS memory—" He broke off apologetically. "There I go, talking technical. That probably doesn't explain a thing to you."

"I've used a computer at work," Karen said, "but I don't know a thing about programming. So I can't keep up with you, except to understand that you're making it work better."

"In a big way," Jeff said. "It'll be a major operation. But I was too busy at the office. I only had the weekends to work on it. So I finally decided to take time off and make one big, concentrated effort. I was due for a vacation, anyway."

She raised her eyebrows. "This is a *vacation*?"

"A vacation is doing what you really want." He flashed her a white smile. "I'd be bored to death on a cruise or something. That's my idea of nothing to do." The smile faded as he continued to look at her, really looking at her now, taking in her cuts and bruises. He seemed to come down from the problem-solving high he had been on.

"How do you feel this morning?" he asked.

She glanced out the window at the gray clouds still scudding above the restless, whitecapped swells that were the remnants of last night's storm. "I had a lovely sleep," she said. She didn't add that she hadn't felt so serene and secure for a long time, for years, not just since the accident. This childhood haven had always embraced her, taken her in and soothed her fears and unhappiness. And yet, to be honest, it was something more than the place, more than this house. She had slept so soundly in the upstairs room because she knew that someone else was there. Someone strong and kind, who had looked into her eyes for one breathless moment....

"You're feeling better, then?" His words cut across her thoughts.

"Yes, much better." Karen turned her gaze toward him, then glanced quickly away again, afraid of revealing her thoughts. She expected him to quiz her on her plans for the immediate future, which were in complete disarray now that the house was no longer available to her. Instead, he stared with hooded eyes at the landscape beyond the window, at the dying fury of the storm. The silence stretched out. She felt a sudden urge to tell him the things about herself that she had so clumsily avoided the night before.

"I want to say that I appreciate being able to stay here last night," she said. "I guess I was in pretty sad shape."

He gave her a quick, unexpected smile. "I'm not quite tactless enough to agree with that. How long had you been traveling?"

"I started early yesterday morning from Santa Teresa, just south of Los Angeles. I took a plane to Portland, and then caught the little bus that comes out here to the coast."

"Are you planning to stay in Nelsmith long?"

She glanced at him, then looked away again. Was that interest in his eyes—or mere politeness? "I have to leave as soon as I'm feeling better, so I can go back to my job. I'm saving my money."

"Got big, expensive plans?" he asked.

Karen regretted her slip but now couldn't seem to lie to him. "I'm having plastic surgery done on my face," she confided shyly.

"But surely your face will heal fine on its own, and there'll be no trace of the accident."

"No, it's got nothing to do with that. I want a nose job," she said bluntly.

"What?" His astonishment was flattering. "Are you serious? Shouldn't you think it over before you rush into something like that?"

"I've thought about it for most of my life." Karen ran her forefinger along the slightly curving line of her nose. "This happened in a fall when I was six years old. I've dreamed of having it straightened for more than twenty years. If my mother had lived, I think she would have understood. But my father always laughed and said that it just added a little character to my face. Well, a young girl doesn't want character—she wants to be pretty. This is the first thing anyone ever notices about me, my crooked old nose. Kids at school used to tease me about it, because they knew it was my sensitive spot. This isn't the first time I've saved up to have it done. I had almost enough in my bank account when I got married. But Edward said—''

"Edward?" he cut in.

"Edward Elway. My husband," she reminded him.

"*Former* husband. He said that plastic surgery is just pandering to an indefensible vanity. So we used the money to buy furniture."

"'Pandering to an indefensible vanity'?" Jeff raised his eyebrows at her quizzically.

"Edward's a college professor. Assistant professor. That's how he talks."

"How long has he been your former husband?"

"Almost fourteen months," Karen said. "I took my own name back, so I'm Karen Grenville again. And I sold that furniture we bought. I've been saving like crazy ever since I got my job, even before the divorce." She ran her finger along the bridge of her nose again. "One of these days I'm going to have it done."

Jeff shook his head, smiling. "I don't know. I think I vote with your father. There's something to be said for character."

She didn't return his smile. Her mind had been made up for too long. It didn't matter what anyone else thought.

Jeff was thinking that she looked absurdly endearing in his old blue bathrobe with the sleeves rolled up. And it surprised him that he should notice what she had on or how she looked in it.

He ought to be back at his computer, following the exciting new path that had opened up for him this morning, not sitting here thinking that even though the long sleep had erased some of the lines of strain from her face, the green eyes were still as large and as sad as they had been before. He suspected that she was about to embark on further mistakes, listen to her aunt, do what others thought she ought to do instead of what was in her own best interests.

He blinked. What the hell was going on? Last night was one thing; it was only natural to offer a little food and sympathy when a shivering stray fetches up at your door like that. Though the lost kitten comparison was not quite as apt as he had first thought. She was not so small or so fragile as he had assumed at first glance. When he had held her against him to calm her incipient hysteria, all that willowy slenderness had been swallowed up by the folds of his extralarge robe, but he had discovered that she was at least six inches over five feet tall. A very good fit for his own six-foot plus . . .

Enough of that. He had to get back to work. This was important time, golden time. He couldn't fritter it away, let himself be sidetracked. On the other hand, he wasn't going to be able to concentrate properly until these distractions were straightened out.

"What are you going to do now?" he asked abruptly.

He saw resignation in her eyes, in her shoulders. "I'll call Minna," she said.

"My car's out back in the garage," he said. "Would you like me to run you into Nelsmith, to your aunt's house? She doesn't have to know where you spent the night."

She shook her head with the faintest of smiles. "As you pointed out, I'm not a teenager anymore. And I was never any good at telling lies."

Karen went quickly to the wall phone, as though afraid that her courage might fail her. There was no answer to the first number she dialed. She dialed again. Jeff refilled his coffee cup and listened openly as she left a message for her aunt.

"Well, what now?" he asked as Karen put down the receiver looking half relieved, half regretful.

"Minna's out showing a house. I left word on her answering machine for her to call me here when she comes back. If that's all right with you?" She looked at him questioningly.

"Of course it's all right. It won't disturb me in the slightest. When I'm working, I never hear the telephone at all."

But he did hear it, about an hour later. Lifting his head from his calculations, he counted four unanswered rings before he pushed his chair back and came out of the back room to investigate.

The kitchen was clean and tidy, with only a faint lingering aroma of cooked bacon to remind him of the meal they had shared. He called Karen's name at the foot of the stairs, but there was no answer. Frowning, he picked up the receiver to still the telephone's insistent summons.

"Yes?" he said shortly.

"Mr. Forrester? This is Minna Grenville. I have a message here to call my niece at the old house. Is that right? Is she there with you?"

"Yes, she's here. Just a minute, I'll find her."

He took the stairs two at a time, with visions of an unconscious form crumpled on the floor nagging at his conscience. Perhaps she was frailer than he had realized. How could the doctors be certain that her concussion was only a mild one? Maybe they should have kept her longer in the hospital. Bunch of quacks...

The suitcase on the straight chair showed him which room she had slept in. His blue bathrobe lying across the smooth bedspread showed that she had dressed and had tidied the room before she left it. But where had she gone?

He took a step closer to the tall narrow windows and caught sight of a slender figure standing motionless on the damp sand of the beach. Her back was toward him as she faced the rolling gray breakers of the sea.

So he had been worried for no good reason. His concern turned to annoyance—with Karen, or with Minna, but mostly with himself.

"Karen's down on the beach," he said into the telephone more curtly than before. "I'll tell her to call you again when she comes in."

"What in the world is she doing up here at this time of year?" Minna Grenville's authoritative tone commanded an explanation.

Jeff declined to obey. "I'll have her call you," he repeated dismissively.

"Wait!" she said sharply. "Whatever possessed her to go to the old house instead of coming straight to me?"

"That's something you'll have to ask *her*."

"Never mind having her phone me," Minna said. "I'm leaving now. I'm coming out there."

Jeff stepped out the kitchen door into the full force of the wind. He raised his arm to wave Karen inside, but arrested the motion as she saw him and started up the path through the beach grass. She came toward him with her head bowed, shoulders hunched, arms crossed tightly across the front of her jacket.

His annoyance strengthened. "Is that jacket dry enough to be out in?" he asked as she reached the door. He realized that the question made him sound like an old grandmother and felt even more aggravated.

"I put it in the dryer while I made breakfast." She straightened up. The wind had whipped a little color into her cheeks. "I thought a little fresh air might clear some of the cobwebs out of my mind."

"And did it?"

"Not really. It was *too* fresh. Too strong—"

"It doesn't help to walk like that, you know," he interrupted.

Her hands stopped in the act of pulling down the jacket zipper as she looked at him in surprise. "Like what?"

"Hunched over, hugging yourself, head pulled in like a turtle. It doesn't really keep you any warmer. It just tells the world that the elements are too much for you. Try it sometimes with your head up and shoulders down. You'll be surprised." Before she could answer, he said, "Your aunt just called. She's on her way over."

"Minna's coming *here*?"

Karen seemed to shrink into herself, and he wanted to tell her again to stand tall and keep her chin up. "Yes," he said. "She's on her way."

Dismayed, Karen put her hands to her windblown hair. "I have to tidy up." She turned away from him and hurried upstairs. Her decision to take the large front bedroom no longer seemed a bold, brave gesture, but merely a presumptuous one.

She looked at herself in the mirror with despair. She was dressed in comfortable dark brown slacks and a sweater, not elegant, but at least unremarkable. But her bruised and cut face looked more damaged than ever.

And Jeff's bathrobe still lay on her bed. She had to return it. She felt a sudden pang as she picked it up. It would be like shrugging off a pair of comforting warm arms around her.... Maybe I'm losing my mind, she thought shakily. She gathered it to her and hurried down the stairs.

There was a sharp knock at the front door.

Jeff came out of the kitchen as Karen reached the bottom step. He started toward the imperious knocking, then stopped and turned back.

"If you'd rather, I'll keep out of this." He lifted an eyebrow questioningly.

"No, no, not at all." Unthinkingly she clutched the bathrobe tightly to her as he opened the door to Minna Grenville.

Jeff's previous words suddenly made sense to Karen as she watched her aunt enter the living room. Head up, shoulders back, Minna Grenville bowed to no weather. Neither did emotional storms daunt her. Her level gaze traveled from Jeff to Karen's battered face, to the oversize bathrobe, back to Jeff again.

"All right," she said directly to Karen. "Begin at the beginning."

Chapter Three

Karen bit her lower lip. The pain in her head pulsed into life again. A sudden weakness in her knees made her sit down abruptly on the chintz-covered couch. "It's a long story, Minna," she said.

Minna bypassed the softer furniture and the maple rocker to choose a straight-backed wooden chair. As tall as Karen, thin to the point of gauntness, she wore her fashionable navy suit with easy assurance. Her gray hair was cut short and smartly styled.

Karen felt young and disheveled in her presence, as always. Even Jeff seemed less formidable under her assessing eye. He looked, Karen suddenly realized, exactly like someone who got out of bed and pulled on the first things that came to hand—the same jeans and sweatshirt he had worn last night. He hadn't remembered to comb his hair, and it curled in dark abandon over his low, broad forehead. He remained standing, one elbow resting on the low mantelpiece as he eyed Minna a little sardonically.

Heartened by the feeling that she had an ally of sorts in the room, Karen plunged into her long, involved explanation. She feared that she would make an incoherent mess of it, as she had when telling her story to Jeff. But this time she wasn't exhausted and half-hysterical. She began at the beginning, with the purse snatching that now seemed like a lifetime ago, and told the rest in sequence.

Minna listened in silence until the end. Then she said, "That bus is supposed to get here no later than eight-thirty at night."

"It wasn't the driver's fault. We had to wait until they cleared tons of mud off the road. You must have heard about it—it happened on the other side of Tillamook."

"You should have phoned ahead to let me know that you were on your way," Minna said. "And I don't know what possessed you to stop at this house instead of coming straight to me."

Karen had already mentioned the lateness of the hour and her own uncertainty of the exact location of Minna's new residence. Neither of these was the true reason, and Minna had recognized them as feeble excuses.

"Oh, Minna, you told me that you bought that one-bedroom place in town because you're sick of everyone you know inviting themselves to stay with you whenever they fancy a few days at the beach. It—it just seemed better all around for me to stay here. I never imagined that you'd have the place rented this time of year."

"The couch in my new living room makes up into a perfectly acceptable bed," Minna said implacably. "And none of this explains why you didn't let me know that you were coming."

Karen felt trapped. She closed her eyes for a moment. "Because I was afraid you might tell Edward," she said at last.

Her aunt's gaze sharpened. "Edward doesn't know you're here?"

"No. And I don't want him to know."

"But he'll be worried."

"Well, I'm not his responsibility anymore, and I wish he'd realize it. I couldn't rest at home because he kept coming around with his flowers and his advice and his kind explanations of all the things I'd done wrong. Starting with leaving *him*!"

"He's only trying to be helpful, Karen."

"It's no help to be constantly treated like a mental and emotional basket case. According to him, I'm incapable of—of crossing the street on my own." Karen knew her voice had started to rise. She put her hands to her throbbing head.

Jeff felt suddenly annoyed at the unevenness of the battle. "You don't seem to realize that your niece has had a concussion," he said. "She needs a little privacy and some rest."

Minna turned to face him. "Are you saying that Karen should stay in this house?"

He met her eyes levelly. "Don't you think that's a decision we could leave up to Karen? She should know whether she wants to stay here or sleep on the couch in your living room."

"Karen," Minna said, keeping her eyes on his, "is that what *you* want—to stay here?"

"Yes," Karen answered faintly.

Minna turned to Jeff. "In that case," she said, "how soon can you move out?"

Jeff caught Karen's involuntary gesture of protest. He shrugged. "No problem. Just find me another house like this one."

"I don't know of another house available right now. But you can have your pick of the motels this time of year."

"That's out of the question," he said. "I can't do my work in a motel, with people coming and going."

Karen said, "Don't ask him to move out, Minna. Please."

Her aunt glanced at her with ill-concealed impatience. "We have to be practical, Karen. One of you has to leave."

Jeff could see that Karen was no match for the older woman. The two of them crowded into one little house was hardly a prescription for quick recovery for the one who was ill.

"Can't we work out some kind of a compromise here?" he asked.

Minna pursed her lips thoughtfully. "I don't see how. Karen can come home with me, or you can go to a motel. Those are the only two choices available."

"I don't think it's quite all that cut-and-dried," he said quietly. "There's nothing to stop Karen from staying where she is, whether I'm here or not. I'm not using any of the upstairs rooms. She's welcome to the whole top of the house." He caught Karen's eye and gave her a reassuring smile. "With kitchen privileges. And living-room privileges—"

"Out of the question," Minna said crisply.

"I do all my work in the back room, so this house will be as private and as quiet for Karen as though she were alone."

"No, it just won't do." Minna stood up and turned away from him, facing Karen.

"You mean that people might talk?" he said to her back.

"Exactly."

"Who's going to tell them? There are no neighbors in sight of this place. That was one of its attractions for me."

"That's beside the point," Minna said crossly. "You don't live here. You don't realize how these things get around."

"Perhaps you'd like to move in and chaperone us." he said. "As I said before, there are plenty of empty bedrooms. Take your pick."

Minna flicked him a brief outraged glance before turning to the couch again. "Karen, get your things. We're leaving."

Minna's gray eyes and Jeff's dark ones both seemed to pierce Karen, each pressuring her to make a decision. She shrank against the back of the couch, searching for some Solomon-like solution that would keep the peace. Often her own mother had similiarly been torn between her strong-willed husband and her equally determined sister-in-law.

The memory of her mother brought with it the memory of her mother's usual solution to family pressure. Karen reached for a convenient throw pillow and lay down on the couch. "I'm sorry," she murmured as she curled up and closed her eyes. Now she was just a wounded casualty, no longer a participant in the battle.

"What is it, baby?" Minna's voice softened for the first time.

"My head hurts," Karen said truthfully.

"She's had a concussion," Jeff sounded *more* angry, not less. "She needs to be left alone to rest."

"I'll call the doctor," Minna said.

"No, don't," Karen said quickly. "I've seen doctors. They say that a concussion is a kind of a bruise, like these bruises on my face, only on the inside. It will go away, but it takes time.'' She opened her eyes a little and regarded Minna through the thick veil of her eyelashes. Her aunt was standing over her, looking uncharacteristically irresolute.

Minna stooped and covered Karen with the first thing that came to hand; Jeff's bathrobe, which Karen had forgotten she was holding. "All right, you rest here," Minna said, pulling the warm robe up to cover her niece's shoulders. "For a day or two," she added, giving notice that though she was retiring from the skirmish, the battle was far from over.

"For as long as it takes," Jeff corrected her.

Karen told herself to lie back and keep still now that her coward's way out was working so well. But the animosity that crackled above her propelled her into further speech. "Don't worry," she said to Minna. "I don't expect I'll be staying long."

They both looked at her sharply.

"I mean, I'll be going back to Santa Teresa as soon as I'm well enough to work."

"You haven't been up here for more than a year," Minna said. "Can't you spare a few days, enough for a decent visit?"

"I haven't taken any time off this year because I'm saving my money, remember?" Karen said hesitantly.

"Oh, *that*." Minna's tone of voice made her opinion plain. "Are you still hanging on to the notion of having plastic surgery?"

Karen nodded without speaking.

Jeff broke the ensuing silence. "Your niece feels that she will be happier if she has her face altered." He spoke in a flat, neutral tone of voice that nevertheless managed to convey his own disapproval of the idea.

"That's nonsense," Minna snapped. "There's no need to go to extremes. Karen, there's nothing the matter with your face and never has been. You've just always had some illusion that a perfect nose would bring you a perfect life."

Karen felt besieged from every side. Why did they both throw obstacles in the way of something that seemed so obvious and necessary to her?

"A nice, normal, straight nose certainly can't make any life *worse*!" she cried. Suddenly heedless, she sat up and threw off the bathrobe. "And don't tell me that I should be satisfied with the face I was born with," she said, running her forefinger along the bridge of her despised nose, an unhappy gesture that had been a habit for twenty years. "This isn't the way it was supposed to be."

She turned to Jeff. "It got like this when I fell down the stairs on an old ferryboat. My father was building a bridge on some forsaken river in the backcountry of Brazil, and there wasn't a decent doctor around when I needed one. That's why it healed this way. So now I'm going to find a doctor to make it right. To make everything right."

Minna looked down at her with an annoyed little shake of her head. "You *do* need some rest," she said. "We can talk about this in a rational manner once you're feeling better." Lips tight, she gave Jeff a severe look. "Do you still have plenty of those frozen dinner things you eat?"

He nodded.

"Then you'll be all right for today. I'll grocery shop for the two of you in the morning." She tucked her smart leather purse more securely under her arm. "Rest now, Karen," she said. "I'll see you tomorrow."

Jeff closed the door behind her, his expression changing to one of faint surprise. "I guess I let your aunt get to me more than I should have. I owe both of you an apology.

That was decent of her, offering to do the shopping. Maybe her bark is worse than her bite.''

"I think it's a little more complicated than that," Karen said. "This way Minna doesn't have to worry that either of us will show up in Nelsmith to attract attention." She started to get up. "I'll see what there is to eat."

He stopped her. "I can stick frozen dinners in the oven as well as the next man. You rest."

Jeff went back to his bedroom workshop after they had eaten. He closed the door to the room behind him, as was his usual habit, shutting himself away from the telephone and other possible intrusions.

His powers of concentration were formidable, making it all the more surprising that thoughts unconnected with computer programming began to swim to the surface of his mind.

He found himself wondering what Edward Elway was like and what Karen had seen in someone who sounded like such a creep. Now *there* was someone who needed his face rearranged....

Jeff looked down at his clenched fist, surprised and a little shocked at his own belligerence. He decided, with a wry grimace, to apply his thinking to the problem he had at hand.

He worked intensely for the rest of the evening. Only, every now and then, his hand would pause briefly on the keyboard and his attention would turn outward, feeling her unheard, unseen presence nearby.

For two days Karen drifted through the house in a lethargic haze. As she moved quietly from room to room, she was constantly aware of his masculine presence behind the closed door. She found herself listening for him, knowing it was foolish of her. His was the kind of intellectual work that made no sound.

She discovered that she was physically tired. Small domestic efforts exhausted her. Now that she was no longer driving herself to work and travel—and fending off Edward's attentions—her tense muscles began to slacken and reveal the depths of their weariness. She could allow herself the luxury of relaxation now that she found herself in a safe harbor, here in this familiar old house. And with someone to turn to for support.

Jeff kept intruding into her thoughts as she fixed a stew for their dinner, a meal that could simmer on the back of the stove and be ready whenever he was ready to leave his cave and come out and eat.

The gray daylight ebbed, and the night came down black outside while she waited for him. Karen built a fire in the fireplace and drowsed in the old maple rocker in the otherwise darkened house. The sound of his step in the hall roused her suddenly, making her heart beat rapidly. She blinked as he snapped on the light.

"I was following my nose to the kitchen," he said. "It smells like you're cooking something wonderful."

By now Karen was so immersed in the rich odors of browned meat and onions and vegetables that she was hardly aware of them.

"Everything's ready," she said, jumping up. "I'll just slide the biscuits in the oven if you'd like to eat now." She hurried ahead of him into the kitchen, turning on lights as she went.

He stopped by the kitchen table, and looked down at the two untouched place settings. "I didn't mean to keep you waiting. You should have gone ahead without me or come back and hauled me out of there."

"I didn't want to disturb you," she said.

"Like I said before, you can disturb me anytime for a home-cooked meal."

Karen thought that it was a pleasant novelty to sit opposite a man with a healthy appetite and no complaints to make about her culinary skills. Maybe she wasn't such a pitiable cook after all. Or maybe he didn't possess Edward's discerning palate....

Though it was not the fault of the food, Karen discovered that she was not hungry. She pushed the stew around her plate, then looked up to meet his appraising eyes.

"You really do look exhausted," he said quietly.

She frowned, annoyed with herself. "I am rather tired, and I shouldn't be. Goodness knows, I've been sleeping enough."

"Maybe a couple of decent nights' sleeps can't make up for a week on the ragged edge," he suggested. "You should just lie around for a few more days until you get your strength back. There's plenty of stew here for tomorrow."

Karen was momentarily distracted by the prospect of a man volunteering to eat leftovers. Then she was even more distracted by the look in his dark eyes as they lingered on hers. There was kindness in them—yes, it must be kindness. Maybe even more than that. Concern? Caring?

His nearness seemed the only reality in the humdrum kitchen, as the rest of the scene faded into insignificance, became insubstantial.

After a moment her gaze dropped back to her plate. She ate a little more. The meal was finished in silence. Not an uncomfortable silence, just a waiting one. It was as though they both could feel something building up around them, something overwhelming, a giant wave getting ready to break. Both of them knowing that it would happen when it would happen, and no sooner. A feeling of anticipation hung like a faint electrical charge in the air.

The telephone rang.

It was Minna checking in. Karen spoke to her briefly, not really disappointed at the interruption as her bone-weariness reasserted itself. This wasn't the right time. But the anticipation stayed with her through the night, woke up with her in the morning.

Jeff continued to work punishingly long hours on his project. Though he had taken to leaving the door to the workroom ajar, she did not disturb him, knowing from his brief explanations that he was nearly to the point where he could wrap it up. Her aloneness could have been lonely, but it wasn't. His presence in the house provided what she needed even more than companionship—reassurance and peace.

And the wave continued to build....

And then one morning Karen woke up feeling healthy and full of vitality once more. Sunshine streamed in at the windows, and the world seemed bright and newly washed. As an outlet for her newfound energy, she made an apple pie for lunch. She served it while it was still hot, and Jeff ate two pieces.

"Better be careful," she teased him, smiling. "You might get fat."

He patted his lean midriff appraisingly. "You may be right," he said. "But I can't pass up real home cooking. It doesn't come my way too often."

That was the first nugget of personal information he had volunteered.

"There's no one at home to cook for you?" she asked, striving to sound casual to hide her burning curiosity.

"Just a cleaning lady who comes in three mornings a week. Sometimes she sticks a casserole in the oven for me—macaroni and cheese, good stuff like that. For the rest, I order in or eat out or heat up some frozen dinners."

That didn't sound like he had a wife or a live-in girlfriend back in California in the Silicon Valley, where all the electronic companies were situated—and flourished. Forrester Software among them. Karen knew that much from talking to Minna, from the information he had furnished when he'd rented the house. Karen pictured Forrester Software as a neat little converted garage, a one-man operation—or maybe two or three—perking along behind a Genius at Work sign.

"I've lived in the same place for ten years, ever since I left college," he said.

She had already guessed that he was somewhere in his mid-thirties. If he'd only been out of college that long, she speculated, he might be a little younger than that. But no doubt he was some kind of prodigy and had finished years ahead of ordinary people. On the other hand he most likely stayed longer and picked up all kinds of advanced degrees. Not like me, Karen thought. I didn't even finish my sophomore year because I couldn't wait to marry my handsome, sophisticated instructor, who knew everything worth knowing and found in me a willing pupil. Too bad I turned out to be such an unsatisfactory one.

Karen poked at a remnant of her piecrust with her fork. She suddenly wanted to know a hundred things about the person sitting opposite her. About his childhood, his school days. His taste in women....

"I just noticed it's a beautiful day out there." Jeff's voice held a note of surprise, as though he was out of the habit of noting what was going on outside these four walls.

Karen followed the direction of his gaze. The view from the window was a breathtaking panorama of blue and gold, of sun, sea and sky. The sky was cloudless, the blue of the sea frilled with the whitecaps of gently breaking waves rolling into shore. Even the deep-throated rumble that was the eternal refrain of the ocean seemed softer than usual.

Suddenly Karen had a feeling of being caged in, walled off from the world outside, thirsty for light and air. On impulse she got to her feet and threw open the window beside her.

The gentlest of breezes wafted in. The merest breath of balmy salt air touched her skin like a lover's caress. It was that rarest of days on the Oregon coast, one without a strong steady wind. Usually the wind would make the flags snap, and kite fliers would have to brace themselves against its pull. This was different—calm. It was a day to be treasured, full of mellow October sunshine and bright with dancing sparkles of light on the surface of the blue water. A day that beckoned them to come outside.

"A lovely day to walk the beach," she said longingly. "All at once I'm sick of being inside."

"That sounds like a healthy attitude to me," Jeff said. "I guess I haven't been out for a while, either. I used to go jogging on the sand every day. Before—" He paused.

Before I came along and upset everything, she finished for him silently.

"—before you jolted me out of my rut and got me thinking on the right track," he continued smoothly. "I'm on top of things pretty much now. I guess I could take a sunshine break." He looked at her questioningly.

"Do we dare to go out?" she said.

He shook his head. "That's up to you. Do you think anyone would see us?"

They both turned to scan the landscape. Minna's house stood in lonely isolation. There were no neighbors close enough to overlook them. The beach itself was empty of life except for a handful of gray gulls scavenging the sands newly uncovered by the outgoing tide.

Karen sighed. "Today I don't care if they do." She made up her mind with uncharacteristic recklessness. "Yes! Let's take a sunshine break, just this once!"

The house stood on a high sandy ridge well back from the water's edge. They went out the back door and walked single file down the side of the dune, following a narrow sandy path worn in the wiry beach grass. The dry sand just above the high-tide line was loose underfoot and made for unsteady walking. They crossed it quickly and reached firmer footing on sand that the ebbing tide had smoothed and moistened to the color and consistency of packed brown sugar.

The air around them was motionless. Karen imagined that an enchanted spell had been cast on them and their surroundings. In silence, side by side now, they turned toward the rocky headland that jutted out into the sea to the north. It seemed to float in a faint golden haze. Nothing in the landscape moved except for the endlessly curling waves, and the two of them. . . .

They fell into an easy rhythm. Jeff's easygoing, loose-jointed stride matched her own, step for step. Karen felt a sudden shiver of happiness sweep over her. She wanted to stretch out her arms and turn her face to the sun and dance circles in the sand. She wouldn't do it, of course. She wasn't that kind of person. On the other hand, she felt a strange shifting inside of her, like the loosening of a lifetime's inhibitions. Could she be drunk on sunshine? There was no denying that intoxicating currents seemed to be swirling all around her, but their source was not the beauty of the day. They came from his silent presence beside her. Her awareness of his masculine aura was so strong that her skin tingled with it.

Karen closed her eyes briefly, not wanting her dazzled expression to betray the chaotic inner feelings that had caught her by surprise. Why now? she thought. Why should all this be happening to her at a time when she was unprepared to deal with everyday life, much less something such as this?

She stumbled and realized she had been walking blindly. His hands caught and steadied her.

"Silly of me." She murmured her apology, feeling half embarrassed, half shameless. Bumbling along like a giddy fool, she had nevertheless achieved the one thing her heightened sensitivity had been thirsting for—the warm touch of his hand on her arm, her waist.

His hand slid slowly down her bare arm, and her pulse leaped shockingly. He clasped her hand in his.

She watched him tremulously out of the corner of her eye as they walked on, more slowly now. What was he thinking, feeling? If only he would say something—anything—she thought. The silence that stretched between them seemed to spin itself into a fine tension that grew as the minutes passed. Finally Karen was propelled into quick, unconsidered speech.

"I love the ocean when it's blue, don't you?" Her words tumbled out nervously. "When the sky lets it be blue, that is. You have to think of the ocean as mighty and powerful, but it's always the color that the sky tells it to be. Gray sky, gray water. Blue sky, blue water..."

Her words trailed off. Jeff didn't answer. She stole a quick sideways glance at him, only to encounter the full force of his dark eyes regarding her with unexpected intensity.

Jeff raised the hand that held hers and pulled her gently toward him. She came unresisting into the circle of his arms. Her own arms went naturally around him, her hands flat against the muscles of his back, her head against his shoulder.

This is everything I've been so desperate for, she told herself. Protection, comfort, strength—

He spoke her name. "Karen..."

She raised her head slowly, almost reluctantly. He bent to lay his cheek against hers. They stood for a moment in an embrace as sweet as a kiss. Then he turned his head, and his lips met hers in a kiss that was less sweetness than fire.

She closed her eyes tight, feeling suddenly at odds with the eerie calm of the outside world. A storm like she had never known was beginning to build inside of her. Her heart was beating so turbulently that she could scarcely breathe. When he raised his head, it was no different. The wild pounding continued, mingled now with his own heartbeats as he held her tightly against him.

Karen slowly raised eyelids grown languid and heavy, turned her head dreamily, and saw a movement in the distance. She stiffened.

"What is it?" Jeff asked.

"There's someone on the beach," she whispered.

Jeff's embrace did not slacken. "Anyone we know?" he said easily.

"I can't tell. It's a man, I think."

"Well, it's a public beach."

Jeff sounded quite unperturbed, but Karen was suddenly overwhelmed by the necessity to remain unseen, to do nothing to incur Minna's wrath. She pushed against him to free herself. For a minute it seemed that he would refuse to release her, then his arms dropped away.

"We have to go back in," she said. "Hurry!" She turned back the way they had come, taking quick long strides that became a half run. She tried to hold back a panic that she knew was unreasonable. Maybe the approaching stranger was just a visitor, not someone who lived close by and might recognize her. Or maybe he wouldn't get close enough to know her, anyway, because she was already at the path up the dune and would soon be safely in the house.

She cast a glance behind her. The stranger was still an indistinct figure in the distance, while Jeff was stalking toward her, displeasure written plainly in every attitude of his body. Her heart sank even as her feet carried her up the slope to the house. Their beautiful moment, and what had she done to it? Torn it into shreds. She wanted to run back into his arms, but he no longer looked the least receptive. And Minna's scandalized voice seemed to ring in her ears. "Kissing on the beach! For everyone to see! Letting everyone know you're living with him—in my house? Couldn't you show some sense—use a little discretion?"

She topped the rise to see Minna's car brake to a stop in the driveway. Karen stopped suddenly. She fought to control her rapid breathing, silently blessing the stranger whose appearance had sent her flying. If not for him, it would have been Minna who discovered them. And what an explosion that would have been. Running away from the possibility of trouble had saved her from certain disaster.

She came forward to greet her aunt. "I didn't expect you today," she said.

"I've just finished talking to Edward," Minna said.

"Oh, Minna! You said you wouldn't—"

"I didn't call him. *He* telephoned *me*," Minna said righteously.

"I suppose you had to tell him that I was here?" Karen felt herself shrinking from the prospect of another, different, disaster.

"Of course. I had to tell him the truth. And he had a pretty good idea where you'd head for, anyway. He's driving up to take you home."

"I'm not going home. Not now. Maybe not ever—"

"Edward can't just pick up and leave his classes. So he'll be here on Sunday, or maybe late Saturday night."

"But he can't. I'm not ready. I don't want to see him. Call him back and tell him to stay away."

"You're the one who should be talking to Edward, not me." Minna's crisp tone did not quite conceal her satisfaction at this new turn of events.

A sudden surprising anger swept through Karen like a breaking wave. Anger at Edward for his refusal to believe she knew her own mind. Anger at Minna for championing his cause. Even some anger at Jeff for choosing to make such a public display of affection instead of a private one that could be savored. But most of all, anger at herself for her inability to deal with any of them.

"Oh, all right." She turned toward the kitchen door. "I'll call him back and tell him myself!"

She punched out the familiar numbers with staccato ferocity. "Edward," she began as soon as his familiar voice came on the line, "this is Karen. I am absolutely not going back to Santa Teresa with you this weekend. Or ever. And you are not to drive up here. Is that understood?"

"My poor little Karen," he said soothingly. "You sound upset."

"If I'm upset, it's because you never pay attention to what I tell you. Just stay away, Edward."

"You'll feel differently in a few more days." The complacency in his voice made her want to scream. "I admit that a more impetuous gallantry would have me drop everything to rush to your side, but I do have a responsibility to my students. Even you would agree to that. So I'll leave you to Minna's care—until Saturday night."

"*Please* don't come," she said a little desperately.

He sighed audibly. "Trust me, Karen. Minna and I only want what's best for you. I'll see you on Saturday." Before she could protest further, he quietly hung up.

Jeff walked into the kitchen while she still held the dead receiver in her hand.

"Your aunt told me that she couldn't stay," he said. "She only stopped by to let you know that your husband is coming up to take you home."

Feeling an all-too-familiar sense of defeat, Karen dropped the receiver back into its cradle. "He's *not* my husband. I wish you and everybody else would stop acting as though he is."

"And why do you suppose everyone does that?" Jeff seemed to take her outburst seriously.

She shook her head. "I don't know why. Edward can't believe that I'm not the same starry-eyed kid I was six years ago. What do I have to do to convince him that the divorce isn't some childish whim that I'll grow out of?"

Jeff frowned thoughtfully. To her it seemed an impersonal frown, as though she had just handed him an unusual word-processing problem. It began to feel as though the interlude on the beach had never happened.

He said, "Are you sure that you're not giving him some reason to think you want to go back to him?"

"I moved out. I *divorced* him. What more does it take?"

"You didn't move very far," he pointed out reasonably. "And have you made any obvious changes in your life-style? Any at all?"

"I'm saving for the plastic surgery," she protested. "Naturally I live frugally, wear the same clothes, look the same. Once I have a new face, he'll have to accept that I'm a different person."

"Changing the outside doesn't necessarily mean changing the inside," he said. "Is it possible that he's right, and a reconciliation is what you want?"

"No, it's not possible!"

"Think carefully," Jeff said. "Are you giving him some reason not to let go? Maybe you're doing it unconsciously."

"*I do not want to go back to Edward.* Not unconsciously or subconsciously or any other way. And I wish you and he and Minna and everybody else would just this once believe that I know my own mind!"

Chapter Four

Just as Karen was warming up to her tirade, the telephone rang. She started, then snatched up the receiver with quick annoyance. How like Edward to intrude at a time like this.

"What is it now?" she demanded.

There was a brief silence on the other end. "Could I speak to Mr. Jeff Forrester?" asked an unfamiliar masculine voice.

Karen felt a hot tide of embarrassment flood her cheeks with heat. How stupid of her to take for granted that any incoming call would be for *her*. She covered the mouthpiece and held the receiver out to Jeff. "It's for you."

She turned to leave the room to give him privacy, but he laid his free hand on her arm to keep her beside him.

"This is Jeff Forrester," he said.

The conversation was about business, much too one-sided for her to follow even if she had been calm enough to try. Had she put Jeff in an awkward position by her thoughtless action? The caller obviously hadn't expected to hear a strange female voice on Jeff's telephone. She moved to free herself, but his grip tightened. The gentle but unyielding pressure of his fingers on her arm only added to her self-condemnation. That touch, that warmth, brought back the memory of the brief heaven of their walk along the beach. The wonder of that breath-less moment—the too-brief moment before she had fled so precipitously...

"Damn it, Tim," Jeff was saying, "I was supposed to have ten more days here. A week, anyway."

Karen's heart missed a beat. He *couldn't* be leaving. Not so soon...

"I know it's an important account." Jeff frowned in concentration. "Look, you and Helen and Mac are qual-ified to draft a proposal. So go ahead and do it."

The sounds from the receiver were still unintelligible to Karen, but she thought she could detect a note of sur-prise added to their urgency.

"That's right, you put it together," Jeff said. "Then fly up here and bring the papers for my signature. *Yes*, I mean it. Okay, I'll see you here in a couple of days."

Jeff dropped the receiver into its cradle with a decisive clatter. "That was Tim Broderick," he said. "Something came up at the office, and he wanted me to come back—what's the matter?"

Karen had stepped back, pulling against his hold. "I *know* Tim. The Brodericks live just down the beach—"

"That's right, he's a local boy. He's the one who told me about this house when I was looking for a place to hole up and work."

"Tim's coming *here*?" she said. "Soon?"

"It should take him a couple of days." Jeff smiled. "And he'll probably need a few extra minutes to pick himself up off the floor and get over the shock of being turned loose to handle his first proposal."

Karen bit her lip as she looked from him to the telephone and back. This day was turning into one disaster after another. She remembered her previous gaffe. "I'm sorry about answering the phone like that," she said.

Jeff made a dismissive movement with his free hand. "It doesn't matter."

"But—Tim might get the wrong idea."

He pulled her closer. "And what idea is that?"

"You know. That I—that you—" She floundered, unable to put the thought into words.

He looked pleased with himself as he drew her into the circle of his arms. "Forget Tim," he said.

For a second she resisted. She felt a brief flash of turmoil, of wanting to cry out against his refusal to listen. Then she let her worries be swept aside as her body molded against his, her head nestling against a broad shoulder. The lovely heart-catching stirrings in her blood were precious new sensations. She sighed and closed her eyes, but the little jeering voice in her mind told her to enjoy herself while she had the chance, because everything would be different once the outside world came crashing in on them.

Tim Broderick would be here in two days. And *Edward* would arrive on Saturday night! The full import of yet another confrontation with her ex-husband seemed to break over her like a monstrous wave.

"What day is this?" she whispered urgently.

"What?"

"What day of the week? I've lost track."

"Hmm." He sounded a little unsure himself. "As near as I can tell, it's a Tuesday. Why?"

Just four more days, and Edward would be here. And they weren't to have even that long to themselves, for now there was Tim. Karen stirred in Jeff's arms. "I'll have to leave."

He only held her tighter. He rested his cheek on her hair. "We're not going to go through all that again, are we?" He said it lightly, but she heard the undercurrent of displeasure in his voice. "I thought we settled all of that with Minna."

She pulled herself away from him, and experienced a pang of misery at how easily he let her go. "But things are different now. With Tim coming, and—and everything." "Everything" was Edward, but she found herself reluctant to say his name, to let him into the room with them, to let the certainty of his pervasive disapproval further cloud this once-sunny day.

"Well, if you're certain that's what you want," Jeff said.

Of course it wasn't what Karen *wanted*. If she could have three wishes, they would all be the same: to stay here and live this morning over forever. From her happy awakening right up to the moment before she sighted the stranger walking on the beach. The rest of the day had brought one problem after another; Minna's visit, Tim's call, the conversation with Edward. If the rest of the world would stay away and leave them alone, how wonderful it could be.

Oh, Karen, how juvenile can you get? She could almost hear Edward's long-suffering voice asking the question. Was she wishing for the moon? She wanted to feel pretty; she wanted to be loved. She wanted to stay here in this house with Jeff. And never, ever leave.

And now she had made Jeff angry with her. Old familiar guilt washed over her. She had spoiled their sweet moments by acting and speaking thoughtlessly. Perhaps that was all they were destined to be—just moments. An interlude. She had been granted a small peaceful time for her inner and outer bruises to heal, and now she was being ousted from her cozy nest.

"Tim won't show up for a couple of days."

Jeff extended this olive branch rather tentatively, but Karen was already mentally packing her things.

"You're going to be busy at your computer," she said. "You won't even notice I'm gone."

"Damn the computer! You're not strong enough to take a steady diet of Minna yet."

Her mind refused to contemplate a move to Minna's house. That would be a long stride backward.

"I won't be going to Minna's," she said quickly.

"Where, then?" he demanded.

She hesitated.

"Are you going to sit in some out-of-the-way motel and stare at the four walls until your husband shows up?"

"My *ex*-husband!" She flung the words at him.

"Answer the question," he said. "Where will you stay?"

She was really being thrown out of her nest now. No Minna, no motel—where *could* she go from here? "I'll-I'll go to the city." She straightened her shoulders, snatching a few shreds of dignity. "To Portland. It's time for me to—to get on with things."

"What things?" he said implacably. "Not that plastic surgery idea you were talking about."

The thought had not occurred to her in the stress of the moment. "I'm not going to do anything like that. I just don't want to be in the way while Tim is here."

He was silent for a moment. Karen thought how nice it would be if he'd contradict her, tell her that she could never be in the way....

"Is that how you're going to handle your ex-husband—just not be here when he shows up?" Jeff asked, putting his finger accurately on her weakness.

Karen turned her back to him, grasped the high back of a wooden kitchen chair for support. The old familiar sensation of being pushed and pressured swept over her again.

The tempting little thought that she really wasn't well enough to cope with Edward yet slid unbidden into her mind. There could be a perverse kind of power in helplessness, as she knew well from her mother's example. The silence stretched out unbearably as she acknowledged the thought—and put it away from her. She straightened her back. "I'll be here when Edward comes," she said.

"Good." The unabashed relief in Jeff's voice surprised her, warmed her. A little of the tension seemed to go out of the air.

He said, "I'm glad you're not leaving."

She had half turned back to face him; now she paused. The situation between them had changed in some subtle but profound way. They had moved beyond that first uncomplicated innocence that had allowed them to share this house in a sort of dreamlike companionship. The kiss on the beach had ended all that. Perhaps she was reading too much into a simple kiss, but even if she misjudged the importance it held for him, she knew that it had changed everything for her.

If she continued to stay here now—in open defiance of Minna, and Tim and Edward and the rest of the world—she would be opening the door to more than a touch of the hand or an embrace on the beach. Much more.

Were they—was *she*—ready for that so soon? Her last relationship had been so badly bungled that she couldn't even disengage herself from it cleanly.

Jeff looked down at her expectantly. She found the courage to take his hand. "Let me go now," she said, "and I'll come back on the bus Friday, after Tim leaves." She searched for approval in his eyes. "That will give you some time alone to work on your program."

"And what will you do?" he asked.

For an instant the prospect of three days in an impersonal motel room daunted her. She forced confidence into her voice. "I can...get acquainted with the city." She hesitated as a new thought occurred to her. "I could read the want ads."

"What?" Jeff asked, obviously struggling to follow her train of thought.

"It's time I started looking for a different job, in a different city." This time her words came out with complete sincerity, taking her by surprise. Just like that, somewhere inside of her a decision had been made. Wherever she went from here, she was never going back to her life in Santa Teresa.

She glanced quickly around the kitchen, checked the time. "I'll do up these dishes and pack. I should be able to catch the afternoon bus to Portland."

Jeff held on to her hand when she tried to withdraw it. "That won't do," he said.

"I *will* come back," she said.

"There's no reason for you to go at all," he said stubbornly.

"I feel that I should go. I'll be more comfortable if I go," she said. "Just for a little while."

"Well, all right. If you're certain that's what you want." The anger went out of his voice. "I'll drive you into the city."

"You don't need to do that," she protested dutifully, but she was unable to suppress a sudden flash of pleasure at the prospect.

"It's only a couple of hours to Portland," he said firmly. "I'll be ready whenever you are."

They drove inland through the fir-covered mountains of the Coast Range with the afternoon sun at their backs. In the dark sameness of the evergreen trees that marched up the steep slopes on every side, maples and birches stood out in bold splashes of autumn reds and golds. The mellowest of October weather held sway. The sun drew up remnants of moisture left behind by the storm, softening the air until it was like balm on the skin and leaving a high blue sky above them that was clouded only by a faint touch of haze.

Karen rode in the passenger seat of Jeff's Volvo in a trance of pleasure, refusing to look forward or back, living in the joy of the moment.

She found it not quite as easy to talk to him as it had been before. Now everything she said had to be first examined and weighed, tested for possible hidden meanings. She was concerned about making a misstep, of seeming to take something for granted that might not really exist. But there was a delicious excitement about it, too. She felt as though she had just discovered a little spring of happiness bubbling away inside of her. She couldn't stop herself from believing that something of importance was happening between the two of them. All this had to mean something—his concern for her, this trip, his insistence that she return. His kiss.

Be quiet. Be careful. Don't make a fool of yourself! The little cautionary voice in her mind clanged its warnings like brass cymbals as the car threaded its way through the hills. But the hiss of the tires lulled it into silence and left her to finish the journey in an untroubled dream.

Their arrival in downtown Portland during rush hour provided a rude awakening.

"Do you have any particular hotel in mind?" Jeff asked as they inched along in bumper-to-bumper traffic.

Karen looked around her in dismay. She had only a superficial acquaintance with the city from occasional trips here when she had lived with Minna. "Maybe we could find something quieter. I saw some motels along the highway on the outskirts of town."

He shook his head. "You don't want to be stuck out in the back of nowhere with nothing to do but watch the grass grow," he said.

"Maybe not. But I don't think I care to be right in the middle of this madhouse, either."

"Things will calm down as soon as all the office workers clear out." Jeff switched lanes dexterously to make a left-hand turn onto a one-way street. "Here's a promising-looking hotel. What do you think?"

Karen thought that it wasn't what she had in mind at all. The Heathman Hotel looked solid and established rather than aggressively new and shiny, but seemed rather more elegant than she was prepared for.

Jeff slid the Volvo into a parking space that a departing truck left open. He reached into the back seat and lifted out her small suitcase. "Let's go."

Karen found herself on a crowded sidewalk. This was the real world, a world where her brown slacks and sweater seemed too shabby to wear into an establishment that boasted a uniformed doorman to usher her through the big glass doors. He was a thin young man with a friendly smile, but she couldn't help feeling that he must be comparing her unfavorably with their usual clientele.

Her suitcase looked small and insignificant as Jeff carried it across the lobby and set it on the floor in front of the counter. "A single room for the lady," he said with easy assurance.

The desk clerk's eyes slid over Karen without pausing. He focused his attention on Jeff.

"A nice room," Jeff added. "Not a broom closet."

The clerk hesitated as though mentally tallying the rooms available, then turned to reach for a key.

Karen suddenly felt like a kindergartner being enrolled in school, standing apprehensive and ignored while the grown-ups conducted their business. She realized that she had unconsciously huddled into herself with her arms crossed tightly across her chest and her head tipped down so that her shoulder-length hair swung forward and shielded her face. No wonder the clerk treated her like the Invisible Woman, she acknowledged wryly. She made an effort to straighten up, and shook back her hair, though it left her feeling exposed and vulnerable.

The clerk turned toward them holding a key, but the motion of his hand was arrested in midair. He was not looking at Karen and Jeff, but beyond them. Karen followed his gaze to where a young woman was walking across the marble floor of the lobby. Karen had a quick impression of an artfully careless tumble of brown-gold hair, a figure-hugging dress in rich autumn colors, long slender legs in filmy nylons and impossibly high-heeled pumps, and a supremely confident bearing. A brief glimpse of a faultless profile left a lasting impression of total self-assurance.

The thought flashed into Karen's mind that someone who looked like that could tell Edward anything, and he would have to accept it. In the next second the woman had disappeared behind the quiveringly attentive back of the young doorman.

The desk clerk's hand resumed its interrupted journey to deposit the room key on the desk. And Jeff also turned his attention back to the matter at hand.

Jeff had noticed the woman, too! Karen felt a sudden wave of loss, of forlornness, even of humiliation. She recognized the unreasonableness of her reaction, but that did nothing to ease her distress. *Of course* Jeff would look at a striking woman; he was human. He was a man. *Every* man in the lobby had turned his head as she went by. Every woman, too, judging by Karen's own actions. And that woman—wherever she was—was probably still continuing her triumphant progress, a steady ripple of turning heads marking her path every place she went.

Karen followed Jeff and the bellboy blindly, her eyes on the carpet, thankful for the curtain of hair that helped hide her face. She would be even more mortified if Jeff should guess what she had been thinking. She had no claim on him, not the faintest right to care where he looked or at whom. What kind of castles in the air had she been building just because someone was pleasant, and kind, and had kissed her once.

She looked around the comfortable hotel room without seeing it. What difference did it make where Country Mouse stayed when she came to town? A broom closet was exactly the place for her—she'd be right at home. There would be the added benefit of having a smaller reckoning to pay out of her carefully hoarded money. More than ever, the vision of a brand-new face danced tantalizingly in front of her. A face such as the one belonging to the woman who had cut such a swath through the hotel lobby. *She* had turned Jeff's head effortlessly.

Karen half closed her eyes, striving to fix that face in her mind.

"Do you want to change before we eat?" Jeff asked.

She stared at him blankly. The brief, remembered glimpse of that coveted profile faded, leaving only the memory of a confident stride, a head held high.…

Jeff raised his eyebrows questioningly.

"Oh," she said, trying to recapture the sense of his last remark. "I—well—do you think you should be starting back? It's a long drive." She was aghast at the words as they came out. She wanted him never to leave. But the prospect of encountering other stylish head-turners, of crueler comparisons, seemed almost more than she could bear right now. Jeff should have someone at his side who looked as though she deserved to be there.

He gave her a slow smile. "I think I can eat some dinner and still be home by bedtime."

Karen felt herself blushing. All the easy congeniality she had once felt between them had vanished as though it had never existed. Now every step took them farther into unknown territory, and every casual remark he made needed to be pondered over, examined for hidden meanings.

He had just made it clear that he expected to spend the night back in the first-floor bedroom in Minna's house. She had wondered a little about that when he had so matter-of-factly accompanied her up to this hotel room. Of course, he had told the desk clerk that she wanted a single. But arrangements could be changed. Perhaps he had looked for some response from her—a meaningful look, some oblique word of encouragement—that would tell him not to leave? Karen had no idea. Suppose she did know some sophisticated signal? Would she dare to use it to keep him with her? She didn't know that, either.

She was no good at this kind of game, never had been. Which was probably the reason that Edward's masterful approach had seemed so wonderfully appealing when they first met. In his view, he would always be the instructor and she the pupil. Not even a very satisfactory pupil, as it turned out. But one who could yet be redeemed if she would only listen to the voice of reason. The voice of reason being Edward's, of course.

Jeff was waiting for an answer.

The sight of her suitcase lying on its side at the foot of the bed saved Karen from having to ask him to repeat the question. Oh yes, he had asked if she wanted to put on some different clothes. The answer to that was simple. She couldn't dress up for him because she had nothing with her any more suitable for city dining than what she had on.

"I don't need to change," she said. "I didn't pack any dressy things when I left Santa Teresa. I didn't expect to need them in Nelsmith." Not that she had anything in her closet back home that resembled what the girl in the lobby had been wearing. She owned nothing so brightly colored and striking—and expensive. "Just give me a minute to freshen up."

She took her purse into the bathroom, where she quickly renewed her lipstick and ran a comb through her air. At least her bruises had faded away. And her hair was clean and healthy-looking, she thought, staring into the mirror with a critical eye, but there wasn't much more one could say for it. It just *hung* there. She pushed it back with her fingers, turned her head from side to side appraisingly. The overhead light seemed to magnify the crookedness of her nose to the exclusion of every other feature. She let her hands drop with a sigh.

"Would you like to have dinner here in the hotel?" Jeff asked as they walked down the hallway to the elevator.

"I think maybe . . . someplace smaller . . ." she said tentatively.

"That will give us a chance to see a little of downtown Portland," he agreed.

As they walked through the thinning crowds, Karen remembered again the uncertainty of that starry-eyed sophomore who had been so easily bowled over by a handsome assistant professor.

She stole a glance at Jeff, striding down the sidewalk beside her. Who would be a proper wife for him? Maybe someone who could entertain important business contacts? Karen felt a small cold shiver at the thought. No, it was more likely he'd need someone to tiptoe around the house and muffle the telephone under a pillow so he could think and not be disturbed. She had already seen what that could be like. If that was what he wanted—

She didn't finish the thought. She didn't know how to finish it.

Jeff scanned the storefronts for signs of a suitable restaurant, and Karen nodded agreement to one that seemed small and dimly lighted. No one looked at her as they trailed the waiter to the last empty table. Not one fork paused in its mouthward journey while its user followed her progress. She had chosen the place because she thought that she could go unnoticed, but, paradoxically enough, she also felt annoyed at being invisible.

She had believed that she'd accepted that situation long ago. She wouldn't have given it a second thought if she hadn't seen that woman walk through the lobby. No—if Jeff hadn't turned to look at the woman in the lobby . . .

Jeff stabbed his fork at his excellent salmon steak morosely, wondering what had gone wrong. This trip was turning out even worse than he had expected.

This morning Karen had been a different person, happy and sweet—and desirable. Like a flower finally daring to open its petals to the sun. The poetic image came unbidden to his mind, surprising him. He wasn't accustomed to flights of fancy equating girls and flowers. He scowled at his plate. Talk about being nipped in the bud. She was as tight and withdrawn as he had ever seen her. Why did she let that pain-in-the-neck ex-husband affect her this way?

"Are you sure you want to stay here in the city?" he said more roughly than he intended. "Why don't we just go and retrieve your suitcase and drive back to the house?"

Karen gave him a quick unreadable glance, then lowered her eyes again. "Please, I don't want to argue about it anymore."

She certainly didn't look as if she was enjoying a minute of this, he thought. What was she going to do when he left—hole up in that hotel room for two whole days? He cast around for some helpful suggestions. "I suppose you could do some shopping," he said.

Another swift look. Another uncomfortable silence.

"I suppose I could." There was no eagerness in her voice.

"Good," he said, putting more enthusiasm into the single word than he actually felt.

They finished the meal in silence.

The sidewalks were comparatively empty when they left the restaurant. The streetlights had come on, each one haloed with a faint nimbus of fog as moisture condensed in the cooling air.

Jeff rammed his hands into his pockets, wondering where to go from here. Everything between them had somehow become prickly and complicated. They had been so comfortable and easy, the two of them together. Like no other woman he had ever met. And now he didn't know what to say to her. And she wasn't giving him any help.

What could they do? Where could they go, the two of them in this unfamiliar city? Perhaps he should go up to her hotel room with her and sit down and talk things out. A quick glance at her rigid profile squelched that idea. Right now she wasn't talking.

And going to her hotel room would probably be the wrong move, too. Come to think of it, it was just after they had reached the hotel that she went all quiet on him. Could she be afraid that he had some idea of spending the night with her there? No, she knew him better than that. At least, she ought to by now. They'd spent days and nights alone together in the house, and he'd never given her the slightest reason to worry about his intentions. Of course, he'd never kissed her before....

He ran his hand through his hair. If only she'd talk to him. What was he going to do with her now? Take her dancing, or something? No, she wasn't dressed for that. Fortunately. He hadn't danced for a dozen years and certainly was in no mood to start again now.

A theater marquee up the street caught his eye. Maybe a movie would be the answer to his problem. It didn't matter what was playing, just as long as they could sit in the dark and not have to talk for a while.

Before he could put this last thought into words, Karen said, "I think you'd better start back to Nelsmith."

"It's early yet," he pointed out, annoyed, sharply aware that this was the second time she had suggested that he leave.

"It's starting to get pretty foggy. The later it gets, the foggier it will probably be between here and the coast. You might run into some bad patches."

He felt slightly mollified at her concern. Now that he had a reason for going, he found that he didn't want to leave. For a brief moment he contemplated getting a room for himself and staying over until morning. The fog would certainly make a perfect excuse. He could get a room on a different floor of the hotel if that would make her feel better. Or even go to a different hotel entirely.

He studied her covertly. Nothing about her gave him the slightest encouragement to linger. Her stance, her attitude, everything about her was as tense and closed up as the first night they met.

"You may be right," he said. "I'll walk you back to the hotel."

He said an awkward goodbye to her in front of the elevator in the lobby. Her green eyes seemed darkly shadowed as the elevator doors slid closed.

Jeff expected to be relieved. Instead, he felt a sudden surprising regret. He should have told Tim to put the damn proposal on hold and let the business wait until he was ready to go back to the office next week. Or the week after that.

Chapter Five

Karen shut the door behind her and flung herself face down on the queen-size bed. The expected tears did not come. Her eyes remained hot and dry, her heart heavy and sore inside her.

She tried to retreat to her old familiar daydream of solving every problem by having a perfect, straight, unbroken nose. She'd be a new and different person.

It wasn't working. She turned over and stared bleakly at the ceiling. Real life wasn't like that. The past few days she had been living in an Enchanted Cottage kind of world. Now fairy-tale time was finished. That woman downstairs had been no fantasy. And Edward was no fantasy.

The reality was that she had until Saturday to transform herself into someone whom Edward would take seriously. And more important, someone who would turn Jeff's head. She was willing to try anything to demonstrate that she was a new and different Karen.

How would she ever do that? Karen brooded over the question as she prepared for bed, and then added a few more sleepless hours to the sum total of those she had already spent on the same unsolvable problem.

In the morning her thoughts turned to a more immediate question. Unless she opted for room service, which would no doubt be incredibly expensive, she had to eat three meals a day in downtown restaurants. All the time feeling shabby and out of place in her just-good-enough-for-the-beach slacks and sweaters. Her apartment closet in Santa Teresa held several neat little wash-and-wear office dresses that would be more appropriate for city streets. Too bad she hadn't thought to pack them.

On the other hand, neat little anythings were not what she craved just now. Last night she had simply ignored Jeff's suggestion that she could spend these two days shopping. Now, getting ready to go down to breakfast, it struck her as not such an outlandish idea, after all. She really would need something new to wear to job interviews once she seriously started job hunting. She might as well shop for clothes now, since she had been plunked down in the center of the city with time on her hands.

Yes, she had plenty of time to spend—but she could hardly say the same about money. Karen reached for her purse and let her fingers rest momentarily on her checkbook. She didn't need to take it out to know to the penny just how much she had in the bank. That total had been the focus of her attention for all these months—no, years!—that she had been scrimping and saving. And she was still hundreds of dollars short of her goal. But...since she was in a situation where she would have to buy something new to wear anyway...perhaps it would be all right to dip into her savings. Just a little... Just this once...

She walked slowly through the noisy downtown streets. Skirting traffic and several construction work barriers, she crossed a central square paved with brick and continued down sidewalks of the same material, oblivious now to the people around her as she studied the window displays of fall fashions.

She eliminated most of the outfits automatically. Too extreme, too bright, too light. Not practical. And, of course, they would be too expensive. She confined herself to window-shopping until she came to a large department store. Then she went inside and straight down to the basement sale racks.

After an hour of fruitless searching, she looked around the little dressing room cubicle in dissatisfaction. She had considered and discarded two different garments, a tan suit and a plain navy-blue dress. They both fit her requirements in every way. Neat, unobtrusive, easy care. And reasonable cost. So why was she returning them to their respective hangers with such definite distaste? In either one she would blend in quiet unnoticeably with the rest of the city's workers. Which was exactly what she wanted.

Wasn't it?

No, of course not, she mocked herself. What I want is to be so drop-dead gorgeous that hotel clerks and waiters—and Jeff Forrester—won't even notice high-fashion blondes whenever I'm in the room.

She shook her head in exasperation. No little navy-blue dress in the world could give her that. Nothing could.

Half angry, half dejected, Karen let the escalator take her upstairs up to the rarefied atmosphere of no markdowns, to price tags so high that she simply refused to check any more prices after the first one. It didn't cost anything to look, she told herself.

Across the aisle from the cosmetics counter, she stopped by a mannequin displaying a sleeveless dress of amethyst silk. Nothing in its perfectly simple lines distracted from the beauty of the fabric.

A saleswoman paused beside her. Karen commented, "It's very plain, isn't it?"

"I imagine it's gorgeous with a real live body inside," said another clerk.

Karen turned and saw that the newcomer had come from the cosmetics department; she carried a tray of emerald-and-silver-colored sample-sized packets.

"Would you care for a free sample of our moisturizer?" the saleswoman asked.

Karen hesitated, then picked up one of the small plastic squares. "Thank you."

"Would you be interested in one of our complimentary professional make-overs?"

Karen took a step backward. "I don't think so. I'm sorry." Even the most elaborate makeup couldn't cure what was wrong with her face. It could only call attention to her flaws. Edward had pointed out that very thing early in their married life. He had been very regretful as he explained it to her, but it was something he felt she ought to know, so he had forced himself to tell her.

"The make-over is completely free." The cosmetics woman was tall with black hair and skin like porcelain. She had a small, straight nose.

"I'm afraid you'd be wasting your time." Karen felt that she should explain. "It's my nose, you see."

"Yes?" The woman looked at her with a puzzled frown.

"It's not—not quite straight." The woman still didn't seem to understand, so Karen plunged on. "I really don't want to call attention to it."

"That's no problem. A good make-over will emphasize your good points—your eyes, your cheekbones and your mouth. You won't even notice a small flaw in your nose."

Karen couldn't believe *that*. Still, she wished with all her heart that it could be the truth rather than just salesmanship. The woman turned and led the way to a tall stool in front of the cosmetics counter, plainly expecting Karen to follow. Karen trailed after her, not in acquiescence, but merely intending to explain the situation more clearly.

The woman gave her a brilliant smile. "I'm Tina."

She stood waiting, and Karen slid tentatively onto the high stool. "I really don't know...."

"Shall we try it and see?"

After all, what was the worst that could happen? If she looked absolutely terrible, she could just go somewhere and wash her face. Karen nodded.

"Just let me pin your hair back." Tina sprayed metal hair clips with something that had a sharp antiseptic smell, then dried them off and secured Karen's hair away from her face. Karen felt exposed and naked. Tina gave her a hand mirror to hold. Karen gripped the handle tightly as Tina began to clean her face with cleansing cream.

"Can you do anything with makeup to make my nose look straighter?" she asked.

"Well..." Tina's hands worked lightly, expertly, as she talked. "Dark contour powder would help to minimize it. But I'll tell you the truth—in my opinion, facial contouring is not very practical. It's more satisfactory to work with your natural features. And this is such a little bump that I'd hate to see you bothering with a contour brush and powder when you don't really have to."

Karen thought privately that Tina wouldn't consider it such a little bump if she'd had to live with it for twenty years. Aloud she said, "Whatever you can do to make it look better—please do it. And show me how."

Tina smiled confidently. "We'll try it both ways, shall we? With and without. So you can decide which you like best."

A teenage girl whose own makeup had been applied with a sure and lavish hand paused to watch them. Karen closed her eyes, retreating into the dark privacy behind her lids. "What is that you're doing now?" she asked Tina presently.

"This is under-eye cream. Concealer. Helps to cover up the evidence of sleepless nights, if you have any. Not that you need it much. Your skin is lovely."

Karen started to shake her head in denial, but the other woman's fingers under her chin held her face motionless. Wouldn't Edward pity her now if he knew that she was clutching at such unlikely straws as under-eye cream and contour powder? She could see his patient smile, hear his faintly chiding voice. "My poor little Karen, will you never learn?"

She stiffened. Why was Edward back inside her head? She thought that she had exorcised him, along with all of his constant oh-so-kind criticism. For a few days, there at the beach, she had felt quite free of him and all his influence. And now he was forcing his way back. No, that wasn't true. *She* was letting him in again. *Inviting* him back. This wasn't Edward's doing; it was her own.

Karen opened her eyes. The teenage spectator was gone.

"What colors do you wear most often?" Tina asked.

Karen hesitated.

"Dramatic colors?" Tina prompted hopefully. She stepped back and studied Karen's face appraisingly. "I can see you in—'' She cocked her head to one side, ''—jewel tones. Vibrant jewel tones.'' There was a hint of a question in her voice.

''You think so?''

''Yes. Ruby, sapphire, emerald . . .''

''Amethyst?'' suggested Karen, letting herself be caught up in the game. Her eyes met Tina's conspiratorially. They both turned to glance at the dress displayed on the mannequin across the aisle.

''Exactly,'' said Tina.

Karen started to draw back to explain that expensive richly colored clothes were not her style. Inside her head, Edward's most disapproving voice instructed her to be sensible. A Country Mouse is supposed to be drab.

Karen took a long deep breath and squared her shoulders. ''Yes,'' she said. ''I'd like to try something dramatic. Well, a little dramatic. If there is such a thing.''

Tina nodded. ''I think . . . violet eye shadow, with those green eyes,'' she decided. She selected lipstick the color of ripe berries.

When Tina finally stepped back, finished, Karen held the mirror up with trepidation. Her eyes seemed twice their size. They dominated her heart-shaped face. And the boldly outlined lips, no longer timidly pastel, were now warm and sensuous. Her crooked nose seemed almost as unnoticeable as Tina had said it would be.

Almost.

''I'd like you to try the contour powder,'' she said.

Tina had been contemplating her handiwork with a smile that conveyed personal satisfaction as well as professional pride. Now a shadow of disappointment crossed her face. ''Don't you like it this way?''

''Oh, yes, I do! It's—it's wonderful! I never would have dreamed—'' Karen broke off to study her image in the mirror again, truly full of wonder at this face she had never seen before. It was exhilarating—and frightening, too, as she realized that the world would expect her to live up to this new exotic countenance. She would need all the help she could get.

"I really want to see it with the contour powder," she said firmly.

She studied her reflection critically when Tina was done.

The darker powder made a small difference. Not enough to win Tina's approval, but enough that Karen felt it would help to boost her own self-confidence. And she would need every ounce of courage she could summon up to wear this face for everyone to see.

Her skin was as clear and glowing as Tina's. She touched her fingers to it experimentally. "It feels so clean—almost as though I didn't have makeup on."

"That is one of the selling points of our product," said Tina, and Karen was reminded that, for Tina, this was a business transaction. For herself it was more like a voyage of discovery.

"What do I need to buy so I can do this for myself?" she asked.

Tina named a dozen articles, from toner and foundation to eye shadows and lipstick.

Karen took a firm grip on her purse. "How much will that be?"

Tina wrote down the individual cosmetics and added up the total. "Two hundred and seventy-eight dollars."

Karen exhaled suddenly, as though the breath had been squeezed out of her. She held up the mirror once more. No, she decided. She'd do it right or not at all. "I'll take everything," she said, half expecting her voice to quaver or break. But it came out quite naturally, as though she made recklessly extravagant purchases every day of her life. "And I'll take the contour powder, too."

Tina released Karen's hair from the metal clips and it swung forward to eclipse half of her newly minted face. Karen shook it back impatiently. "I'll have to do something about this," she said, reaching a decision without second thought. "It spoils the effect."

Tina nodded. "If you'd like to visit a beauty salon, there's one on the fourth floor. I go there myself."

With a firm hand, Karen wrote out a check for the amount of the bill. Then she went upstairs to make an appointment with the hairdresser.

All the way back to the hotel, Karen lingered in front of shop windows, seeing only as far as her own reflection in the glass.

She was light-headed, almost giddy, with a breathlessness that was half apprehension, half triumph. She had done something far more drastic than applying—and buying—unaccustomed makeup. This was not something that could be cancelled out with a little soap and water. For the first time since childhood, she had short hair.

Short and feathery, shot through with blond highlights, brushed up and away from her face, it was no longer a neat chestnut screen to hide behind, to shield her from the world.

As she arranged her purchases in a row under the mirror in the hotel bathroom, her hands paused in midmotion, and she stared at herself again. Once more her emotions ran the full gamut, starting from sheer disbelief, melting into cautious acceptance, a flash of unaccustomed pride—then plunging straight into panicky denial.

Did she really look better? Or was she simply making a complete fool of herself? She had truly burned her bridges this time, even going so far as to break into her precious savings. She was stuck with this face for an indefinite length of time.

She listened for Edward's familiar scolding voice to sound within her head. Instead, Jeff's image slid into her mind. She could see him plainly, see those dark intelligent eyes, those eyes that would soon scrutinize her, judge her. What would she see in those eyes? What would he think? That she had made herself ridiculous?

She realized that she was standing with the jar of moisturizer cream still in her hand. She put it down with unnecessary firmness. Jeff had turned to watch the girl in the lobby, hadn't he? So therefore he must like curls and cosmetics on a woman. And fashion and color. And self-confidence.

The telephone on the bedside table shrilled into life, startling her out of her reverie. She ran to answer it, a tide of pleasure sweeping over her. Only one person in the world could be calling her here.

"Karen?" The sound of Jeff's voice sent a small shiver up her spine. "How is everything going?"

"Fine. Just fine," she said in a rush. She sat down on the bed and composed herself to speak more calmly. "Did you run into much fog on the way back last night?"

"A few patches here and there. Nothing much." There was a small awkward pause before he spoke again. "How about coming home tomorrow?"

Her heart missed a beat at the word. Could he possibly share her feeling that "home" could be wherever the two of them were together? No, she mustn't make the mistake of reading unintended meaning into a mere figure of speech.

"Tomorrow?" she said. "Won't Tim Broderick be there tomorrow?"

"Yes, he's catching an early flight from San Francisco to Portland, and then he'll rent a car to drive out to Nelsmith," Jeff said. "If you're ready to come back, I thought you could catch a ride with him."

The last thing Karen wanted was to spend two hours in a closed car with a curious ex-schoolmate while trying to explain why she was sharing a house with his boss! And looking like this!

"I don't think that would be such a good idea," she said. "I'll stay here until he leaves. How long will he stay?"

"I hope to get him headed back sometime on Friday. It depends on how much backlog has piled up since I've been gone."

"Oh." Karen tried to keep her disappointment from coloring her voice. "I thought he was just bringing you a few papers to sign."

"That was the original idea," he said. "But it turns out that there are other things waiting for my decision, so we might as well clear up whatever's pending. Are you sure you don't want to come back tomorrow?"

"Yes, I'm sure." Remembering her manners, she added, "But thank you for thinking of me." *Thinking of me, he's thinking of me,* sang a bubbling little voice inside of her.

"I'll drive in and get you once I'm done with Tim," said Jeff.

Karen was pleased by all this solicitude on his part, but she wasn't entirely certain that she wanted to be considered quite so helpless. "The Beach bus runs twice a day. I can take that."

"We'll see," Jeff said firmly. "When I call you tomorrow, I should have have a better idea of when I can get rid of Tim."

In the morning it took her more than two hours to du-
plicate Tina's work of the day before. Karen's unprac-
ticed hand was unsteady and tentative.

"I should have learned all this ten years ago," she
muttered under her breath, remembering the glossy teenager who had paused to watch the make-over for a brief
time yesterday. At that age Karen already had her eyes
firmly fixed on plastic surgery as her only resource, and
she had shied away from anything that would call attention to her face as it was.

At last she stepped back and lifted her chin at her reflection in the mirror. It seemed that even the brown
slacks and sweater appeared a little less dowdy than they
had the day before. Karen half turned, and looked over
her shoulder to study her image. Yes, it was true; even her
clothes looked different. Perhaps because she was standing straight and holding up her head. Almost as though
she was staring back at the world with defiance.

Her posture seemed to be saying, "If you don't like
what you see, that's *your* problem."

Karen felt herself wilt a little. It was easy enough to be
brave in the isolation of her hotel room, she thought. It
would a different story out on the city streets.

She would have to keep reminding herself not to duck
her head, now that her comforting screen of hair was
gone. She caught her bottom lip between her teeth in
sudden dismay, then hastily released it before she could
spoil her lipstick. This face was going to take a lot of living up to. Especially since she was well aware that it was
not the new, perfect face she'd dreamed of, but the same
old one, slightly camouflaged.

She crossed her arms tightly in front of her as if to hold
herself together and protect herself from all the eyes that

would look at her and dismiss her with indifference. And from the eyes that would never see her at all.

No, she had to stop that, too. Holding her arms down stiffly at her sides, she watched the woman in the mirror gradually lose her bravura like a balloon leaking air. She worried at her lower lip again, then had to break off her critical study of her image in order to make repairs to her lipstick.

"This just isn't going to work," she told her reflection. "If I have to concentrate on how I look and walk and hold my head every minute, pretty soon I'll be too self-conscious to put one foot in front of the other." She needed something to take walking with her. "What goes walking with the beautiful stylish models in advertisements?" she asked herself. "Besides a handsome stylish man," she added ruefully. How about a beautiful stylish dog? she thought. A tall silky Afghan hound, perhaps. If she had an imaginary Afghan on the leash, maybe she would automatically stand tall and hold up her head to avoid disgracing the animal.

She tried walking around the room with an invisible pedigreed hound pacing at her side, laughing at herself a little shakily yet finding the bonds of tension begin to slacken. Quickly, before she could chew off any more of her lipstick, Karen went out and shut the door behind her.

Down the blessedly deserted hallway and in the empty elevator, she elaborated on her fantasy charade. The dog's name, she decided, was Otto von Something Something. Such an aristocratic dog deserved a noble name. "Heel, Otto," she said silently as the elevator door opened.

The short distance across the marble floor of the lobby was traversed without incident. The young doorman smiled at Karen with such goodwill that she smiled back

involuntarily and then walked straight-backed down the
street with an unfamiliar feeling of lightness.

She felt the smile lingering on her lips as she played out
her goofy game of invisible dog-walking. She thought that
if the oblivious passersby could hear what was going on
in her head, it would be a straitjacket she'd wind up with,
not a nice, new suit of clothes.

Sometime during the night she seemed to have made the
decision to buy herself an entire new outfit. And not in a
bargain basement, either.

One great advantage of imaginary dogs, Karen thought
cheerfully, is that they can be left outside department
stores for indefinite periods of time without causing their
owners any worry or guilt. "Stay, Otto," she murmured
under her breath, and still smiling, pushed open the heavy
glass door.

She began by looking at tailored suits. She had in mind
a plain navy or black skirt and blazer, a good blouse,
perhaps a bright scarf. But her attention kept straying to
other departments, other styles. Bright-patterned sepa-
rates, draped skirts, unstructured jackets or formfitting
ones caught her eye. And—above all—rich colors. "Vibrant jewel tones," Tina had said. These were all of that;
deep glowing purples and greens, wines and blues. Pea-
cock colors.

Her final choice was a compromise: a slim skirt and
loose jacket of fine wool in a purplish-red color the saleswoman called mulberry. She also selected a long-sleeved
silk blouse and brilliant matching scarf that splashed a
rainbow of color on the rich, dark mulberry back-
ground. All for a price tag that took Karen's breath away
once again. This time she hesitated only slightly before
reaching for her checkbook.

She bought new shoes, black pumps with slender heels—high heels, now that she had no need to remember that Edward was on the short side and expected her to feel as sensitive on that subject as he did.

To complete the ensemble, she selected a good black shoulder bag of fine leather, fine workmanship and a fine large price tag. Karen stroked the smooth leather with her hand and didn't flinch at the cost.

Then, her shopping complete by every practical consideration, Karen went back and bought the little amethyst dress.

It fit her like a dream. The subtle curves of the dress skimmed her own, lending a smooth silken flattery to her narrow waist and the swell of her hips and breasts. Karen turned from side to side in front of the fitting-room mirror. No mundane consideration of price or usefulness penetrated her dreamlike state. She seemed to have no more will than a sleepwalker. Like a sleepwalker, she wrote out a check for another breathtaking sum and then gathered her purchases and floated down to the main floor on an airy cloud.

As she stepped out onto the street, reality struck her like an icy deluge.

Had she lost her mind? All that money for a dress she didn't need and would never get an opportunity to wear! Pedestrian traffic eddied around her as she stopped dead in the middle of the brick sidewalk. Stores and offices were closing; it was rush hour again. She looked back irresolutely. The department store would be closing soon. Too late now to go back and correct her mistakes. She clutched her packages more tightly and began to trudge down the street. Her newfound self-confidence seemed to be such a thistledown thing that the least breath of adversity blew it completely away.

She had even forgotten about Otto.

Karen straightened her shoulders once more. "Come on, Otto boy," she murmured through clenched teeth, "I really need you now."

Back in the security of her room, Karen hung the dress on the padded hanger that the saleswoman had put in the bag. Limp, with neither mannequin nor human body to fill it, the garment looked hardly worthy of passing notice. Paradoxically that very unassertiveness rekindled some of Karen's original desire to own it. It was as though the dress and she shared a delicious secret. Separately they were easily overlooked. But together—

"Together—*what*?" she said aloud, crossly. "Together we rule the world?" She put her hands to her head. "I wonder if I really am out of my mind? Maybe that concussion was worse than I thought."

No, she was just doing things she had never done before—and scaring herself a little silly in the process. Talking to herself. Talking to imaginary *dogs*, for heaven's sake. Still, she shouldn't cast aspersions on poor Otto. Goodness knows he had managed to take her mind off herself while she ventured into strange new worlds.

After she redid her makeup, Karen dressed carefully in her new suit and sat down to wait for Jeff's promised telephone call. Tonight she would eat in the hotel dining room. Alone. Each time she thought of that, she readjusted the bright scarf around her neck. Over the left shoulder, over the right, knot in the back, straight down in front...

Appetite had almost conquered nervousness by the time the phone rang. The call was late. The news was not what she wanted to hear.

Chapter Six

"Tim's here with me," Jeff told her. "We're still working."

A pang of disappointment shot through Karen, sharp enough to surprise her. What had she expected? A long cosy chat? Followed by some rosy plans for tomorrow? Her conscious imaginings had only gone as far as picturing herself walking in the front door of the beach house, resplendent in her new finery. And Jeff's face when he saw her...

"How long...?" She couldn't finish the sentence.

"We'll get done tomorrow for sure." Jeff sounded harassed. "He brought a stack of things for me to take care of. I'm up to my neck in paperwork. I go away for a couple of weeks, and the whole place grinds to a stop!"

"That's...too bad." Karen chewed on her lower lip. She didn't want to seem insistent, but she really needed to know when Tim would leave. The Beach bus only made two trips a day from Portland to the coast. The first one would get her there around noon, the second not until eight-thirty at night. Another unhappy thought struck her. Tomorrow was Friday, the end of the work week. "About Tim," she said hesitantly, "I wondered if he's planning on staying in Nelsmith over the weekend."

"Why would he do that?" Jeff sounded puzzled.

"Well, it sounds like he hasn't had much opportunity to visit his parents. And I thought he might like to spend a couple of days at the beach now that he's here."

"No way! Tim has to get back to San Francisco and get busy straightening things out." Jeff sounded as though the concept of the weekend as a time of leisure was entirely alien to him.

"Look," he said, "you just stay where you are, and when Tim leaves I'll call you and drive in and bring you back."

Karen stirred uncomfortably. It was wonderful of him to take it for granted that he should come and get her. He certainly wouldn't be making the trip because the bright lights of the city held any attraction for him. If he came, it would be because of her. So why didn't she feel entirely delighted at the prospect?

"Well . . ." she said to fill the lengthening silence.

"I'm sorry I can't tell you what time we'll be through," Jeff said. "Early afternoon, probably."

She thought that she could detect fatigue in his voice. No doubt he'd been forgetting to eat and sleep regularly. He sounded a little constrained, as though Tim might be within earshot. He also gave her the feeling that he was impatient to get back to work.

She made a quick decision. "You have enough to think about without worrying about picking me up. I'll just get on the bus and come on out. That will be simpler for both of us."

Now it was his turn to hesitate. "You won't be walking down the road at night like you did before?"

"No, of course not. That mud slide was just a freak accident." Without taking time to think she added, "Anyway, I'll take the early bus. So I'll be sure to get there in daylight."

Karen sat by herself at a table for two in the hotel dining room, experiencing fewer qualms than she had expected. She wasn't sure whether any of the other diners had noticed her walk in or not. Between remembering to hold up her head and being careful not to meet any stranger's eyes, she had found herself seated and studying the menu before she had time to worry about whether she was being ignored.

The food and service were both admirable, but she paid little attention to what she ate. She had too much to think about. Tomorrow loomed in front of her like one huge question mark.

To put it in the bluntest, most embarrassing terms imaginable—where was she going to sleep tomorrow night?

Without a doubt, Jeff expected her to spend the night back at the beach house, to continue on as they had begun. It certainly would never occur to him that one kiss might change everything. She had felt completely relaxed and guiltless staying in the house with him during those days when they were just friends. Now, with the possibility that they might become more than friends, it no longer seemed so simple, or so right.

She could always go to Minna's, of course. That might be best. Only it would be awkward to explain it to Jeff....

And then there was Edward. He would be showing up sometime during the weekend. Karen didn't want to think

of him at all. So she didn't. It was surprising how easy it
was to put him out of her mind. She had much more immediate worries to occupy her time.

The small Beach bus left Portland bus station less than
half-full. Karen leaned back in her window seat and
closed her eyes briefly. She had a few hours left to make
her decision, the one she hadn't been able to arrive at
throughout the night. She hardly noticed the bus turning
onto the freeway that led out of town. If only the alternative to the beach house were something easier to contemplate than the couch in Minna's living room. She
thought again about going to a motel, but she already
knew Jeff's opinion on that. He would see it as a form of
hiding. And maybe he'd be right. Maybe it would be another way of avoiding a decision, not facing up to the real
world.

She was as well prepared to face up to things as she had
ever been in her life. This morning she had searched for
reassurance in the eyes of strangers—and found it. Both
the hotel clerk and the young doorman had been aware of
her presence in a way that was more than mere professional politeness. More than one pair of masculine eyes
had lingered in her direction longer than strictly necessary. The taxi driver had done everything but whistle.

Her new facade was a clever disguise, a suit of armor;
she might be quaking inside, but the rest of the world
could only see the outward reality. No one needed to know
that she propped up her courage by walking with an invisible Afghan hound.

If a person needed to have an imaginary dog, she
thought ruefully, one thing to be said in his favor was that
he was easy to travel with. Even a tall elegant fellow the
size of Otto took up no room on the bus. And he most

obligingly evaporated into thin air whenever he wasn't called for. Karen lowered her lashes a little guiltily. Fantasy was all very well in its place, but it wasn't likely to do her much good when she got to Nelsmith and had to face Minna.

The implications of her last thought made her open her eyes wide again. Apparently she had made up her mind— and had decided to stay with her aunt. She began at once to rehearse what she would say to Minna, and to imagine what Minna would say to her. She switched her scarf from one shoulder to another, caught a point of the bright silk between her thumb and forefinger and began to roll it up and flatten it out again.

After a few moments she became aware of what she was doing. The rest of her body was still, but her busily working fingers were broadcasting her agitation for anyone with eyes to see. Relaxing her hand, she smoothed her skirt over her knees, let her fingers come to rest on the cool leather of her new purse. These were the reality, the things that would have to help her through the coming interview. This time she couldn't rely on Otto.

She got to her feet as the bus braked to a stop at the center of Nelsmith's one long straggling business street. The little town stretched out in the shelter of a long ridge, which protected it from the worst of the ocean gales and muted the perpetual roar of breaking waves to a dull undertone. The houses and shops had the weathered look common to all but the most prosperous of seaside communities. The tourist season was well over for this year, and the street was nearly deserted. Karen carried her suitcase past a T-shirt shop and a candy store with Closed signs in their windows.

Minna's real-estate office was comprised of two tiny rooms in a little gray-shingled building with Grenville

Realty lettered on its single plate-glass window. Photographs of houses and typewritten Property for Sale notices taped to the window almost obscured Karen's view of her aunt working at her well-worn desk.

Karen set her suitcase down outside the door, tilted her chin at an uncomfortable angle and stepped inside.

Minna looked up casually, then sat upright in surprise. *"Karen?"* she said.

Karen said nothing. Minna pushed back her chair and came around to the front of the desk. "Karen!" she repeated, brushing the sleeve of the mulberry jacket with her fingertips. "For a second I didn't even recognize you. Where did all this come from?"

"From Portland. I just got off the bus." Karen saw a flash of something that might have been relief in Minna's eyes, but it was gone before she could be sure. "I suppose you know that Tim Broderick came up to work with Jeff for a few days."

"I heard that Tim was in town," Minna said dryly. "I wasn't informed of the reason."

Karen realized that her aunt had been picturing the three of them, Jeff, herself and Tim, all staying together in the big isolated house. If that were true, it would have provided enough fuel to send a regular brushfire of gossip crackling through the town behind Minna's back.

"I went to Portland as soon as I heard that Tim was coming," she explained quickly. "And while I was there, I bought some new things."

"You certainly did." Minna subjected her to an incredulous scrutiny that took in every detail from shoes to hair. "You actually spent some real money for a change. Whatever inspired you to do a thing like that?"

Karen hesitated. It was too complicated for easy explanation. "Part of it was because of Edward," she said

THE JOKER GOES WILD!

Play this card right!

See inside!

IT'S A WILD, WILD, WONDERFUL

FREE OFFER!

HERE'S WHAT YOU GET:

1. *Four New Silhouette Romance™ Novels—FREE!*
   Everything comes up hearts and diamonds with four exciting romances—
   yours FREE from Silhouette Reader Service™. Each of these brand-new
   novels brings you the passion and tenderness of today's greatest love
   stories.

2. *A Lovely and Elegant Gold-Plated Chain—FREE!*
   You'll love your elegant 20k gold electroplated chain! The necklace is
   finely crafted with 160 double-soldered links and is electroplate finished
   in genuine 20k gold. And it's yours free as added thanks for giving our
   Reader Service a try!

3. *An Exciting Mystery Bonus—FREE!*
   You'll go wild over this surprise gift. It is attractive as well as practical.

4. *Free Home Delivery!*
   Join Silhouette Reader Service™ and enjoy the convenience of previewing
   six new books every month, delivered to your home. Each book is yours
   for $2.25*. And there is no extra charge for postage and handling! If
   you're not fully satisfied, you can cancel at any time, just by sending us a
   note or a shipping statement marked "cancel" or by returning any
   shipment to us at our cost.

5. *Free Newsletter!*
   It makes you feel like a partner to the world's most popular
   authors . . . tells about their upcoming books . . . even gives you their
   recipes!

6. *More Mystery Gifts Throughout the Year! No joke!*
   Because home subscribers are our most valued readers, we'll be sending
   you additional free gifts from time to time with your monthly shipments—
   as a token of our appreciation!

GO WILD
WITH SILHOUETTE®TODAY—
JUST COMPLETE, DETACH AND
MAIL YOUR FREE-OFFER CARD!

IT'S NO JOKE!

MAIL THE POSTPAID CARD AND GET FREE GIFTS AND $9.00 WORTH OF SILHOUETTE NOVELS—FREE!

If offer card is missing, write to:
Silhouette Reader Service, P.O. Box 1867, Buffalo, NY 14269-1867

slowly. "I couldn't stop him from driving up here, but I thought that if I looked different, more—more competent, or something—that he might for once pay some attention when I tell him we're finished." She knew that this was not at all what Minna would like to hear.

Perhaps this was as good a time as any to find out if her new outer facade was convincing to the eyes of someone who knew her well. She stepped back and extended her arms slightly out from her sides, inviting appraisal. "What do you think?"

Minna's austere face was quite unreadable. "Turn around," she said.

Karen rotated slowly, chin raised, inwardly braced for the scathing criticism that her aunt had so freely dealt out in the past.

"I think you need some nail polish, in a color that matches the suit," Minna said finally. "Otherwise—it's perfect."

"Oh, *Minna*! You *like* it?" Karen reached out to the older woman. Minna embraced her. They held each other tightly. "You really like it?"

"You look wonderful." Minna's eyes were suspiciously bright as she stepped back. "You've *always* looked just fine to me. And to your father. We never could understand what all the fuss was about. How many times have we told you—" she checked herself abruptly, then started over again using a more conciliatory tone. "Never mind that. You did say that you just came in on the bus?"

Karen nodded.

"Well, let's go to the house, and I'll fix some lunch. I'm alone here today. I'll just lock up the office until I get back."

The sight of Karen's suitcase propelled Minna into speech again, quick scolding words. "For goodness' sake, Karen, you left your suitcase outside on the street."

"That's right, I did." Karen picked it up and fell into step beside her aunt without further explanation. Not taking it in with her had been an instinctive decision, not a calculated one. Now that she looked back on it she supposed that she had wanted the first encounter with her aunt to be as uncluttered as possible. Just the two of them, with no additional questions, such as where she would be spending the night. Time enough to go into that later. But not now, not just yet.

Minna gave her a quick sharp look. Karen tried to meet her gaze with an expression both noncommittal and pleasant, but her pulse quickened at the sudden tension between them.

Minna defused the situation by looking away. For a few moments they walked in silence down the quiet street. Then Minna glanced back at her appraisingly. "We're the same height, for a change," Minna said. "I haven't seen you in high heels for years."

"Edward felt it was disloyal of me to wear anything but flats."

Minna snorted. "Disloyal? What a word to use."

"That was his way of putting it." Karen tried to keep any trace of resentment out of her voice. She had never made a practice of coming to Minna with domestic complaints, knowing in advance on which side her aunt's sympathies would lie. Minna would always see Edward as the adult and Karen as the child in their relationship. Not that she could really blame Minna too much for that—for a long time Karen had believed the same thing.

"Edward is not a small person," Minna objected. "Even high heels wouldn't make you taller than he is."

"Not quite," Karen agreed. "But they did put us nearly on the same level, and that made him feel very uncomfortable. It was easier just to wear the lowest heels I could find."

Minna's lips tightened. Karen waited for her usual caustic comment, but the moment passed and Minna said nothing.

There were many such pauses in their lunchtime conversation as each of them recognized—and steered away from—tiny verbal precipices that held the potential to drop them back into their previous strained relationship. Karen found it rather like walking on eggs, picking her words with such care. But the situation was not entirely unpleasant. The knowledge that Minna was also struggling, trying to treat her as an equal, made the experience a positive one.

Karen admired the convenience of the almost-new small house and the coziness of its location, sheltered as it was by the hill behind it.

"But don't you miss the ocean view?" she asked curiously.

"I've looked at the Pacific every day for thirty years." Minna moved efficiently around the compact modern kitchen. "Any time I feel the urge to see it again, I can walk up to the top of the hill. And I don't have to walk back down to a monster with five bedrooms and a bunch of leaky gutters."

There was a moment of awkward silence after this oblique reference to the house on the beach. The question of where Karen would be spending the night lay between them, a question that had the power to blow away all of this cautious amity.

Karen knew that if she would ask, "Can I stay with you?" the answer would be "Yes." But saying it would be like surrendering much of her newly won territory and admitting that Minna had been right.

And Minna hadn't been right. Nothing could have been better for Karen than those days—and nights—in the beach house with Jeff. Nothing else could have been so healing, so life-giving. It was just that now the situation was changed. What had been so simple and right had become complicated, fraught with unknown possibilities.

Minna finally tackled the subject that was uppermost in both their minds. Carefully avoiding Karen's eyes, she glanced around the snug brightness of her little kitchen and said, "I'm sorry I don't have a guest room anymore."

Karen picked up her cue gratefully. "The couch in the living room will be fine for me." As though by mutual agreement, the subject was dropped. The conversation turned to local gossip and other safe topics.

When Minna glanced up at the wall clock some time later, Karen stopped in midsentence, surprised that so much time had gone by. "I'm keeping you from the office," she said.

"There's no hurry," Minna replied. But she began to clear the lunch things from the table. "Do you have plans for the rest of the day?"

Karen got up to help her. "Yes," she said, carefully not looking at her aunt. "I'm going out to the beach house." It was hard for her to ask, but she kept her voice even as she said, "I need a ride. I thought, before you go back to the office, you might drop me off out there."

Minna was silent long enough to make Karen think she was framing a refusal. Finally she said, "Yes, you obviously can't hike three miles up the road dressed like that. And in high heels. You can drive yourself. Take the Buick. I won't be needing it today."

* * *

Driving up the coast road, Karen tried to discern the motive behind Minna's unexpectedly generous gesture. Was giving her the use of the car Minna's gruff way of saying, "I'm on your side now. Go with my blessing."? Did she want Karen to have freedom of movement, to be sure that she could get home without relying on Jeff Forrester? Or did she still resent Jeff so much that she wouldn't drop Karen off herself because it might look as though she endorsed this visit? Karen could see that she still had a long way to go before she would understand her aunt.

She braked the car halfway up the long sandy driveway. Jeff's Volvo was nowhere in sight, but was probably parked in the big garage at the back of the house. She waited for a moment, almost expecting him to come bursting out the front door. Don't be silly, she told herself. If he's working, concentrating, he'd never hear a car engine. That wasn't in the script of her daydream, anyway. In her imagination she would open the door and Jeff would turn and see her—the new her! And then—? What came next was still hazy, but she was sure it would be wonderful. Almost sure.

Karen stirred a little uneasily as she released her grip on the steering wheel. The dream had seemed so real. Now that she was here, doubts assailed her. Maybe he wouldn't like the new Karen. She reached for a mirror for reassurance. Her eyes looked wide and frightened. She shut them tightly and tried to summon up her courage. Over the trip-hammer pounding of her heart, she whispered, "Come on, Otto, walk with me as far as the front door."

Then she remembered she hadn't put the house key back in its usual hiding place. Oh, well, the daydream would play out just as well if Jeff came to the door and found her standing there....

She knocked sharply three times and waited. There was no answer. She knocked again. Jeff must be in the back room, working. Suddenly the bolt snapped back.

"Hi." A sleepy-eyed Tim Broderick looked at her without recognition.

"Tim?" Her disappointment was too sharp and unexpected to hide.

He studied her more closely *"Karen?"* he said in the same surprised tone that Minna had used. "Karen Grenville? You look great! Come on in. Are you back to visit the old homestead?"

Karen glanced hastily around the room and was relieved not to see Jeff. Her daydream had never included the presence of a third person. "I didn't expect to find you here, Tim," she said.

"I guess you know all about Jeff Forrester, my boss, renting the place to finish a job he's working on." Tim kept talking as he walked backward in front of her, his eyes never leaving her face, his own face registering equal parts of admiration and astonishment. "I heard from my folks that this house was empty. So I told Jeff it was the perfect place for his vacation. Isolated and quiet—and far enough away so the people at the office couldn't expect him to drive back to San Francisco every time a problem came up. It was just what the doctor ordered."

Karen wasn't about to confide in Tim Broderick how much she knew about his boss's arrangements. "And where *is* your Mr. Forrester?" she asked.

"In the back room at the computer. We're working." Tim ran the fingers of both hands hastily through his rumpled fair hair. "Well, Jeff's working. I was just taking a nap on the couch. Sit down, Karen. I'll get us a cup of coffee."

Karen followed him into the kitchen. Tim awkwardly poured the coffee while keeping up a steady stream of chatter, scarcely taking his eyes from her face even yet.

So much for all her elaborate fantasies, thought Karen. She dropped into a kitchen chair and laughed a little at her own folly.

"What's funny?" he demanded.

"Nothing, Tim." He frowned a little, and she felt she had to say more or risk offending him. On the other hand, she could hardly tell him the truth. "I'm thinking that you've just said more words to me than you did in the whole two years we went to the same high school." Tim had been a popular boy, bright, athletic, good-looking.

Tim's face reddened a little. "No fair, Karen. You were a couple of years behind me. And how was I to know you were going to turn out so gorgeous?" He took the chair across the table from her. "Come on, tell me all about yourself."

Karen sipped her coffee. "I thought you said you were working. I wouldn't want to interrupt anything important."

"You can interrupt me any time you like. It doesn't matter." Though the words were playful, his tone was not.

She raised her eyebrows questioningly.

"Whatever I do, he'll do over again, anyway." Tim jerked his head toward the back of the house. "We've spent the last two days working on a bunch of stuff I brought from the office. I also brought along a proposal he gave me the go-ahead to draft by myself. Now he's started checking on *that*, making sure I did it right."

"*Did* you do it right?" she asked.

"You bet I did. And that's exactly what he's going to find, even if he spends the whole weekend going over it."

The whole weekend. Karen's heart lurched. "He won't do that, will he?"

"Who knows." Tim slouched back in his chair and stretched his legs out into the middle of the room. "Don't get me wrong. He's a great guy. Practically a genius in his field. Only that field doesn't happen to be business administration, if you know what I mean."

"I'm not sure that I do," she said.

"Well, once you've got a bunch of employees working for you, the secret for getting the work done is to make sure somebody else does it. I tell him, 'Jeff, you've got to delegate, delegate, delegate.'"

"But suppose nobody else can do the job?" Karen couldn't keep from defending Jeff's position even though she suspected that Tim was right.

"Nobody else is ever going to get a chance to learn how, as long the top man does it all himself."

It was fascinating to see this other side of Jeff, to have this glimpse of him through the eyes of a third person. Tim described a Jeff who was almost a stranger to her. Not entirely, though. She had seen a little of Jeff's capacity for immersing himself in his work. Tim must be able to tell her a hundred things about the man he worked for, things she was hungry to know.

Tim broke open a package of sugared doughnuts that was lying on the table, offered it to her, then took one himself when she shook her head. Karen wondered briefly what the two of them had been eating here on their own.

Tim polished off the first doughnut and helped himself to another. "You're not living in Nelsmith anymore, are you?" he asked.

"Not for half a dozen years," she said. "I've been living down in southern California. I just came up for a visit."

"Yeah, I keep telling myself I ought to come up and see my folks every fall, when the weather is so good, but somehow I never seem to make it."

Karen didn't want to make idle conversation about herself or the weather or anything else. She wanted to listen to him talk about Jeff. She searched for a way to tactfully turn the conversation in the direction she wanted it to go. Tim could be a positive mine of information if she just picked the right tools to open him up.

Realization of what she was doing swept over her suddenly. Tim wasn't aware that she and Jeff already knew each other; he never would talk to her so frankly if he did. It wasn't fair to pump him, to lead him into saying things he might not say if he knew the true situation.

She put down her coffee cup. "I've been in Portland for a few days," she told him. "Before that—last week—I met Mr. Forrester. Jeff."

Tim's warm camaraderie sharpened into wariness. The temperature in the kitchen seemed to drop a few degrees. "You know Jeff Forrester?"

Karen started to bite her lower lip but made herself stop. It was plain that Jeff hadn't spoken about her to Tim. Maybe he hadn't thought of her while she was gone. Maybe he didn't remember those few lovely days as constantly as she did. "Yes, I know him," she said, leaving the statement purposefully vague.

Tim clammed up.

She had done the decent thing, by protecting Tim from too much unguarded frankness. She had also cut off her rich source of inside information. He wasn't going to tell her the things she wanted to know. Worse than that, any minute now he was going to wake up to the fact that she hadn't offered him any explanation for coming here to this house. She wasn't about to say that she had come to see Jeff. For a moment all of her being was concentrated on sending a silent message: "Please, Jeff, please come out of that back room before I say or do something that will embarrass us both!"

Jeff raised his eyes from the computer screen to the blank wall beyond. Something had been nagging at his attention for the past few minutes. There it was again. Voices. His eyebrows drew together in a frown. Surely Tim had better sense than to turn on a radio and disturb the quiet while he was back here trying to concentrate. He tried to go back to his calculations, but the sound was as pesky as a mosquito in a dark room.

He pushed back his chair and got to his feet. It was time for a stretch, anyway. And maybe a cup of coffee. He walked down the long hallway, the ancient boards underfoot creaking at each step. Stopping in the kitchen doorway, he took in the scene in front of him with one long penetrating glance.

Tim and his ever-present package of doughnuts took up one end of the table. At the other end, framed in the light from the window, sat Karen. A Karen who looked at him with eyes that were bigger and greener than he remembered them from before. Pale sunlight haloed her head. She looked different, too different for him to take in all at once.

Part of it was the way she was dressed. He hadn't seen those lovely slender legs in sheer nylons before. And the suit she had on was pretty—and fashionable, too, he guessed. He felt a faint uneasiness somewhere inside of him. Somehow he hadn't thought of Karen as being fashionable.

But the difference in her was more than just the way she looked. It showed in the erect way she held herself, in the tilt of her head. This was not quite the same Karen who had come to him like a bedraggled kitten out of the storm. Not the same Karen he had kissed on the beach.

He became aware of their eyes on him, expectant, waiting for him to speak. He stepped inside the room. It was a large, old-fashioned kitchen. Karen was, perhaps, ten feet from him. At this moment, somehow, it seemed that there was more distance between them than that.

Chapter Seven

"Hey, Jeff, look who's here," Tim said. "Karen and I went to high school together."

For Karen the magic moment was broken, her daydream ruined. She could *kill* Tim Broderick for being here, for trampling over her surprise with his big, clumsy, oafish presence! It was all the more infuriating that he hadn't the slightest idea of what he had done. She tried to conceal her flaring anger, but couldn't keep a slight edge out of her voice as she spoke. "Don't give Jeff the wrong idea, Tim. Back then you were Mr. Popular, and I was just that skinny little Grenville kid. You didn't know I was alive."

"And that just goes to show that the best of us make mistakes," Tim countered cheerfully. He became more serious as Jeff turned to help himself from the coffeepot. "Speaking of mistakes," he said, "how is that proposal looking to you, Jeff?"

"What?" Jeff said, distractedly. "Oh, that. I don't know yet." His eyes came back to Karen.

She felt the full weight of his gaze, his attention. He liked what he saw; she was almost sure of that. If only he could tell her so....

"Did you walk all the way down from the highway?" he asked.

"No, I drove. I've got Minna's car."

Jeff's eyebrows went up a little. "Minna's car?"

Karen went on quickly. "I took the bus into town. Minna said—well, when I asked her to drop me off here at the house, she said she didn't need the car the rest of the day, so she just gave me the keys."

And a fine mess I just made of that explanation, she told herself silently. Now Jeff's standing there wondering what's going on, why Minna is back in the picture. And I can't tell him any more right now—not with Tim sitting across the table from me.

She certainly couldn't explain to Jeff that she intended to stay at Minna's tonight—and why. That was going to be difficult enough to do once they were alone. If they ever were alone, she thought with annoyance. There was very little that either of them could say without arousing Tim's suspicions that something was going on between them. Not that it would be the end of the world if Tim decided that Karen and his boss were interested in each other. But she and Jeff should have a chance to discover just how deep that interest went before letting an outsider in on the situation.

Jeff switched his thoughtful gaze from her to Tim. "Have we cleared up all the paperwork you brought with you from the office?"

Tim nodded.

"The whole works? There's nothing left?"

"Just the proposal. All the rest is ready to go."

Jeff was silent for a moment, deep in thought. With sudden decision, he said, "About that proposal. Do you have confidence that it's right the way it is?"

Tim straightened in his chair. "I'd bet a bundle on it."

"In that case, I'll put my money on it, too. Send it in as it is," Jeff said. He paused. "Maybe you could just check it through one more time before we button it up."

Tim looked at Karen for a split second, then his eyes flicked away. "Okay, sure. I see what you mean. Good idea." He left the kitchen quickly.

They waited silently, listening to the sound of his receding footsteps. The workroom door slammed loudly.

Karen's eyes met Jeff's. "I don't think you can call that an angry door slam. It sounded like a tactful one to me. I'm afraid Tim thinks that—that something is going on."

"I'm sure he does." Jeff put down his untasted coffee and came toward her. "Tim's supposed to be a bright boy. I'd be disappointed in him if he couldn't see what was right under his nose." He reached out, took her hand and drew her to her feet.

"You don't mind?" She spoke a little breathlessly.

"About what?"

"About Tim."

He shook his head briefly, as though brushing aside the whole subject of Tim. He looked down at her. "You cut your hair," he said.

Suddenly it was hard for Karen to breathe. Her daydream was coming true at last. "Do—do you like it?"

"It looks nice." As though aware of the inadequacy of his response, he touched a wisp of curl at her temple with the tips of his fingers. "You look . . . different."

Yes, she said to herself, I've made myself into some-one you might turn to look at if I were a stranger. Of course, it's not quite the real me. Not yet . . .

He drew the tip of his finger down the side of her face, lightly tracing her cheekbones, the curve of her cheek. Her skin seemed to come alive at his touch. A little fountain of happiness bubbled inside Karen, leaping higher at each touch, steadying at that higher level, holding there—waiting for the explosion of his kiss. Karen closed her eyes as the fingertip brushed first her upper lip, then the lower one, leaving behind a tingling awareness. She felt light and boneless. It seemed completely natural to relax against him as his arms encircled her.

For a long blissful time they stood motionless in a si-lent embrace. As he continued to hold her close against him, she remembered what it had been like during that one precious moment when the two of them had come together on the beach. They had been completely ab-sorbed in each other, as though the rest of the world had ceased to exist. She didn't feel that same single-minded concentration on Jeff's part this time, nor was there quite the same abandon in herself.

Jeff spoke slowly. "For a place so isolated that there's not a neighbor within half a mile, a person has a hard time finding any privacy around here to—to—"

He didn't need to finish the sentence. Karen knew ex-actly what he meant. Out of sight was not quite out of mind, for they both were acutely aware of Tim's presence in the house.

Jeff closed his eyes momentarily as he held her close. Yes, he thought, she felt the same in his arms. It was the same Karen, sweet and desirable, just as before. But when he opened his eyes again, it was a different Karen that he saw. Not a less desirable one. More conventionally desirable, if anything. Surprisingly lovely, and fashionable and poised. But someone unfamiliar to him. She was not the vulnerable, heart-catchingly helpless young woman his sympathies had gone out to.

As he stared at her face, her long, dark lashes trembled against her cheeks, and her eyes opened slowly, dreamily. That clear green gaze held him mesmerized for a moment.

"You look—different." He said it again, because the thought was uppermost in his mind.

She smiled a little ruefully. "It's not even skin-deep, I'm afraid. A little soap and water and I'll be right back to the old me."

Jeff shook his head. That wasn't quite true. The real difference was in the way she stood, and walked, and held herself. Tim had noticed it, too. Jeff had seen the same look on his office manager's face often enough before. Not the lingering surprise, but the glint of awakening interest. Known throughout the company as the office Romeo, Tim was considered a connoisseur of women. Jeff had to admit that Tim hadn't been wrong to sit up and take notice of Karen. *This* Karen. The one who seemed like a stranger in his arms.

Their previous relationship had felt simple and natural. A comfortable familiarity had let them open themselves to each other without any of the artificial conventions such as dating and dinner and searching for topics of conversation. *His* Karen might still be in there somewhere, hidden by this attractive packaging, but right now he wasn't sure. And that uncertainty left him oddly off balance.

"Tim's going to stay in the back room until I go and haul him out," he said. "The sooner I do that, the sooner he'll be on his way."

While Tim packed his things and confirmed his early-morning flight from the Portland airport, Karen watched contentedly out the kitchen window as a bank of fog crept over the water half a mile offshore, making a dark streak across the horizon. The setting sun changed into a glowing red circle as it dipped beneath the edge of the fog.

When the last suitcase had been loaded into the rented car, she got to her feet and went into the front room to say a polite goodbye to Tim. Only to discover that Tim had come up with a different idea.

"Do you realize that Jeff hasn't had a decent meal since he's been here?" Tim asked her.

She looked past him quickly to catch Jeff's eye. Jeff smiled and lifted both hands helplessly. Karen turned her attention back to Tim, feeling a little glow inside that she and Jeff shared small secrets.

"He hasn't had one good seafood dinner since he came to this house," Tim was saying. "Every time I ask him if he's been to this place or that place, the answer is always no. Now that the work is finished, the least you and I can do is take him out and make sure that he eats something besides sandwiches and frozen dinners."

Karen shook her head. "I don't know, Tim." When she was a lonely sixteen-year-old, she never would have believed that the day would come when all she wanted to see of Tim Broderick was his back going out the door.

Jeff stepped in. "Don't worry about me, Tim. I'll manage just fine."

"Come on, Jeff, I insist. Do it for Karen's sake," Tim said. "Just look at her. She isn't the kind of girl you can ask to eat pizza in the kitchen."

Karen suppressed the sudden urge to laugh aloud. Tim couldn't guess how far off the mark he was this time. She glanced at Jeff again to share the joke, but his eyes were on Tim and his expression was serious.

Frowning a little, Jeff said, "I suppose we do have to eat. How far do we have to drive to find one of these restaurants you're talking about?"

"Just a few miles up the road. Five or six. And then you can eat great seafood and have a view of the ocean."

"We'll have a view of the fog bank, more likely." There was no enthusiasm in Jeff's voice. "I suppose I'll have to get dressed up for this."

"Only as much as you feel like," Tim said diplomatically. "No neckties." He had on an open-necked knit shirt and a well-tailored sport jacket. Jeff was wearing his usual sweatshirt and jeans.

Jeff disappeared into his bedroom to change, and Tim turned to Karen, grinning. "This is quite an achievement, getting Jeff to go out on the town. As a rule, wild horses couldn't drag him to any kind of a social affair."

"Really?" Karen was doubtful. Jeff hadn't seemed shy or reclusive to *her*.

"Oh, he suffers through a business dinner occasionally, but anyone who knows him can always tell that half his mind is working on his latest program."

Jeff came back freshly shaven, wearing a good-looking sport coat, and, by organizing their dinner, proceeded to demonstrate that he was capable of thinking of other things besides business.

"Karen will come with me in the Volvo," he told Tim. "There's no point in you coming back to the house, so you drive the rental car, and then you can leave for Port-land right from the restaurant.''

This arrangement was eminently sensible, but Karen's thoughts immediately leaped ahead to the time when Jeff would have to drive her back here to the beach house to pick up Minna's car. She'd had no opportunity to ex-plain to him just why she wasn't coming back to sleep in the big upstairs bedroom, and she wondered uneasily once more how she was going to do that, what she was going to say. And how he would react.

He didn't give her any opening to discuss it on the short drive up the coast road to the restaurant. He was disap-pointingly silent all the way. Karen told herself that nei-ther of them could be expected to relax and be natural until Tim was finally out of the way for good.

They lingered late over their excellent meal. Tim made a most entertaining host, and Karen found herself join-ing in his bantering talk as easily as though she had never been the shy little wallflower she was so used to consid-ering herself. Part of her newfound ease came from not having the slightest romantic interest in Tim Broderick. Part of it came from having Jeff sitting on the other side of her. Her pleasure might have been heightened in small part by the single glass of wine she had with dinner, but its effect was negligible in comparison with the confi-dence she felt that both men were pleased to be seen with her, to show her off.

Karen was particularly gratified that, while Jeff lis-tened more than he talked, he showed no impatience, no inclination to cut short the conversation, and never once steered it back to the subject of business.

Jeff was satisfied to let the other two discuss high-school days and old friends while he sat back and watched them. He thought there was a sparkle about Karen that came from inside and had nothing to do with how she was dressed.

That sparkle definitely had not been present before. Or was it just that he hadn't noticed it? Could he have missed it during those long days when her peaceful, undemanding presence had become an accepted part of the atmosphere of the old house? No, the Karen who had crept into his mind and his thoughts during those days had been a fragile creature. Someone who had needed his help badly. Who somehow had managed to distract his attention from the very job he had come here to accomplish.

Jeff marveled silently at how swiftly he had abandoned his work once she had announced her intention of going to Portland. After these past two days of being once more totally immersed in business, he could hardly recognize in himself the Jeff Forrester who had so impulsively dropped everything to run off to the city. Something had been happening to him back then, had been changing him. Tim's coming had interrupted that change, had brought him back to cold reality.

Reality seemed cold indeed to him as he watched Karen and Tim exchange laughter-tinged reminiscences of their school days. He felt left out, a little dull, as he often felt in social situations. Small talk had never been his strong point. Though he hadn't had any difficulty in talking to Karen before she went away. Talking to the other Karen.

Could it be Tim's presence that brought out this difference in her? Though Jeff watched them sharply, he could see no flirtatiousness in her attitude toward him, no significant glances, no warm looks. And when Tim glanced at his watch and said regretfully that he'd better be on his way, Karen agreed with him promptly. So promptly that Tim looked a little taken aback.

Once Tim was gone, silence fell between the two of them. It was not a comfortable silence, such as those they had shared in earlier days, but one full of unspoken questions and strangeness and doubts.

Finally Karen spoke. "I'm going to stay at my aunt's house tonight. I—I told her I would. And I have to take her car back to her."

Jeff reached for his coffee cup to hide his surprise. And his brief jolt of relief. So they were going to have a breathing space, he thought. A little time to get reacquainted before—before what? he wondered.

When he put down the cup and looked over at her again, she seemed more tense, with her hand clenched in the discarded napkin beside her plate.

"I guess that's all right," he said slowly. "As long as you feel in shape to be dealing with Minna."

"Oh, yes. I'm all recovered from the concussion. Even the headaches are gone."

"That's good."

There didn't seem to be anything else left to say. Jeff's previous feeling of relief began perversely to change to annoyance. "You aren't coming back to stay at the house, then?" he said.

Karen started to bite her lower lip. She made herself stop. That was the big question, wasn't it? And she didn't have the slightest clue what the answer would be. There were too many unknowns. Did he *want* her to come back to stay? And if she did—then what? What would she be coming back *to*? A brief affair? That held not the slightest attraction for her. If she gave herself to anyone ever again, it would have to be wholeheartedly—both on her side and on his. After a long pause, she said tensely, "I'll be over early tomorrow. I—I can make your breakfast."

That was hardly an answer to his question, but it was the best she could do at the moment.

He frowned briefly, then nodded his head. Karen exhaled a shaky breathy of relief. What if he had said not to bother? Said that he was tired and planned to sleep late? There was no denying that he looked worn-out. His eyes were hooded with fatigue. She knew without asking that the past days had been filled with long hours of work and very little rest.

The ride back up the coast road was a mostly silent one. The fog bank was making landfall. A thin white mist shrouded the road and turned into pearly luminescence in the headlights of the Volvo.

When Jeff switched off the motor and the lights in the driveway, the fog made the darkness more absolute. It muffled the sound of the waves on the beach below them. He turned the lights back on. The moisture in the air diffused the beams, made the world seem dreamy. For a moment, neither of them stirred.

"Maybe you shouldn't try to drive to Nelsmith in this fog."

"It's not that bad," she reassured him. "I'll be fine." If it had been a little thicker, the fog would have provided a solid excuse not to go. But Karen knew that she had to leave—unless he took this opportunity to say all of those things that would make it possible for her to stay with him.

Minutes ticked by. Jeff did not speak, did not reach out to touch her. The chilly dampness of the night began to penetrate the interior of the car.

Karen opened the car door and stepped out into the wiry grass at the edge of the driveway. Jeff had parked well to one side in order to leave room for her to back Minna's Buick out onto the road. The Volvo's headlights lit her path to the other car. She heard the door on Jeff's side of the Volvo slam shut. He caught up to her in swift strides. As she opened the Buick's door, Jeff caught her wrist, turned her to face him. Wordlessly he gathered her into his arms. His lips found hers in a long hard kiss that had a touch of desperation in it.

Karen's heart leaped, then settled into an irregular pounding. She clung to him tightly. This was no slow-building wave of bliss that she felt, but a sudden fierce desire that sent tremors through her body.

He released her at once. "You're shaking. You're cold."

Before she could deny it, he was holding the car door open wide for her. Lazy tendrils of fog wreathed around the two of them, brushing Karen's face with damp, chill fingers. She shivered for real this time. His hand touched her shoulder, guided her into the Buick.

"Drive carefully," he said.

She looked up at him. Her lips, which had been burn-ing a few minutes ago, now seemed frozen. She had to try twice before the words would come out. "I'll—I'll see you for breakfast," she said finally. "About nine o'clock?"

He nodded and stepped back. "Until nine o'clock," he said.

The dashboard clock said eighteen minutes past eight when Karen drove Minna's Buick up to the beach house in the morning. The fog was beginning to lift, and she could see as far as the first line of breakers offshore. The waves were tumbling gray-white and milky under a pearl-gray sky.

She let herself in the front door. Her sneakers made no noise on the floor as she carried two full grocery bags into the kitchen, feeling a little like Cinderella on the morning after the ball. Jeans and T-shirt and her serviceable blue jacket made yesterday's triumphs seem like a dream.

The house was completely still as she began to unpack the fruits of her early-morning shopping trip. She set out eggs and the other ingredients for a special omelet. Some items went straight into the refrigerator to wait for the night: a very thick steak, mushrooms and salad greens. Last of all, she tucked two long white candles into a drawer. Her little amethyst dress was hanging, shrouded in plastic, in the car. Tonight she would serve a perfect romantic candlelit dinner in front of the living-room fireplace. And she would be Cinderella all over again.

She tiptoed carefully down the hallway to the open door of Jeff's bedroom. He lay on his side, facing her, one shoulder and arm uncovered, his breathing deep and even. Some of yesterday's tired lines had smoothed from his face, but traces of fatigue still remained.

Looking down on him, Karen felt a great yearning tenderness, an overwhelming desire to take care of him, to shield him from all the demands of the world. She stepped closer, hand outstretched to pull up the blanket around his bare shoulder. Before she reached the edge of the bed, she came to her senses. Suppose he woke up and found her like this, standing over him, tucking him in? How embarrassing. For them both.

She stood motionless for a moment. The ticking of the bedside clock, the loudest sound in the stillness of the room, intruded into her consciousness. Frowning, she picked it up, turned it over and saw that the alarm button was pulled out. Turning it back, she saw that the alarm was set for eight-thirty. Any minute now it would go off and wake him up. Karen pressed the button in firmly before returning the clock to the nightstand. There was no reason to interrupt Jeff's much-needed sleep just because she had unthinkingly named nine o'clock as the time she would arrive. She smiled fondly. Breakfast could wait. *She* could wait.

Back in the kitchen, she stood in front of the window, gazing dreamily at the gray ocean. That kiss last night had made all the difference, dissolved all her doubts. Now anticipation was singing in her veins. She felt too restless to stay quietly inside and look at the view. She reached for her old blue jacket. As she went out the back door, she told herself that at the very first opportunity she would buy an all-new outfit for walking the beach. And it would be the boldest, brightest color she could find. Raspberry, maybe. Or fuchsia.

The thought of shopping reminded her of Otto. Dear Otto, she had left him high and dry on the front porch yesterday afternoon. He hadn't crossed her mind once since she took leave of him and stepped through the front door to test out her newfound confidence in talking to Tim.

She smiled at her thoughts as she made her way down the sandy path to the beach. *I must be turning into a Hard-Hearted Hannah, abandoning a faithful hound like that.* On the other hand, maybe it was a sign of good mental health not to need an imaginary dog in order to cope with everything that turned up. Karen shook her head slowly. She didn't believe she would ever need to re-sort to that kind of a prop again. She had something—*someone*—much better. Better than a whole menagerie of make-believe animals. Someone real.

So this was a farewell. A goodbye to Otto. She didn't have a reward to give him. He was hardly the type to sit up for a dog biscuit. But all dogs love to run on the damp sand below the high-tide mark. Maybe he would enjoy one last romp.

She was walking north along the water's edge, facing into the faint breeze that stirred the slowly lifting fog, thinning it to reveal half-recognizable shapes and then hiding them again. It was the perfect setting for a tall, ghostly hound to go stretching his legs, joyously racing back to Neverland.

"You're free, Otto," she whispered. "Run. Be happy. Goodbye."

Seconds later, a few hundred yards ahead, a scavenging seagull flew up from the tide's edge, squawking as though something had disturbed its feeding.

"Sic 'em, Otto," Karen said.

She smiled gently at her own folly as she strolled along with her hands tucked in her jacket pocket.

Sea sounds filled the air around her. The roar of the surf was muted by the fog, but still all pervasive. She couldn't remember ever being so happy.

"Karen!" A familiar voice called her name.

She turned to see Edward striding down the sand toward her. "Karen." His voice was stern. "I've just come from the house. I suppose you realize there's a man in there. In bed. Sleeping."

Chapter Eight

"*E*dward?" Karen's voice was full of disbelief. She felt totally surprised. Not so much at his presence—but surprised at herself that she had temporarily forgotten all about him.

"What's going on here?" he demanded. "Who is that man?"

Karen refused to let his impatience rush her into speech. As he covered the remaining distance between them and came to a halt in front of her, she looked at him, but directed her attention inward—to her own feelings. Or to the lack of them. There was no sick emptiness in the pit of her stomach—her normal reaction to that tone of voice. She felt no frantic rush to placate him or to justify herself.

"Well, Karen?" He folded his arms and stared at her, frowning.

She noted irrelevantly that he was wearing his favorite tweed jacket, the one with leather patches on the elbows.

He was always at his most professorial with her when he wore that jacket.

Facing him with her feet planted in the sand, her hands in her pockets, chin tilted, she said, "I hope you didn't make a lot of noise and wake him up."

He gaped at her.

Now it was her turn to frown. "What were you doing inside the house, anyway?"

"Looking for you, of course." Edward pulled himself to his full height and recovered his equilibrium. "I knew you were staying at the old place, so I came straight here."

Karen felt a momentary impulse to rush in with a quick nervous explanation of the true situation to let him know she'd spent the night at Minna's. Then she reminded herself that she no longer owed Edward an accounting of her actions. And, in this case, he had some explaining to do himself.

"I didn't expect you to get here so soon," she said.

"*That* is only too obvious."

Edward's lips thinned into a straight line as he waited, apparently expecting her to rise to this bait. When she remained stubbornly silent, he said, "I found someone to take my Friday class. I've been on the road for nearly twenty-four hours, driving straight through without stopping for sleep."

For a fleeting second, Karen felt the way she used to feel—guilty and apologetic for putting him to so much effort. Then her new, stronger self recognized that Edward had planned it that way. He was weary, and she was supposed to accept that it was *her* fault. He knew her so well—her lack of confidence, the way she hated loud voices and arguments, the lengths to which she would go to avoid a confrontation of any kind.

She trembled a little inside. With an effort she kept her voice firm and steady as she said, "In that case, you had better check into a motel and get a good sleep before you turn around and start back to Santa Teresa."

Edward smiled. The tolerant, patronizing, pitying smile that once had reduced her to tears of frustration. "Come now, Karen, let's not play games. We both know there are half-a-dozen empty beds in that big house. Not even counting the one that your 'friend' happens to be snoring in at the moment."

Karen nearly blurted out that Jeff did *not* snore, but she saw the trap in time. Edward expected her to say just that and then to fall apart with embarrassment when he asked her how she knew. A tiny flame kindled inside her. She hated anger—and feared it—both in herself and in others. But this time she let the fire grow enough to warm herself with its heat.

Speaking slowly and distinctly, she said, "You're not welcome in that house, Edward. You wouldn't be welcome even if Minna hadn't rented it out to someone else. The person you trespassed on this morning happens to be her latest tenant."

Edward's fair skin reddened a little. "A likely story," he snapped, uncharacteristically losing some of his composure.

Instead of retorting in kind, Karen let his remark go unanswered. She braced herself inwardly and tried to assume the expression that he habitually used on her at such times. Raising her eyebrows slightly, she attempted to look both patient and superior. Apparently she didn't do it well enough. Edward gave her a quick searching stare, but he recovered his aplomb with no visible effort.

"You've cut your hair," he said accusingly.

Karen clenched her fists inside her jacket pockets. It was so typical of Edward to drag in a totally irrelevant criticism of herself whenever an argument wasn't going entirely his way. If only she could have faced him yesterday, armored in her new clothes and her newfound confidence. Instead of like this. All she had now was her new makeup, and she had applied that with a very light hand this morning. I can't do this on my own, she told herself a little desperately. She needed her expensive new suit. Her high heels to make her as tall as he was. And Otto to remind her to stand tall.

Once again she felt the impulse to rush into speech, to argue, to explain. She deliberately made herself turn away from him to gaze out at the gray-white foam of the breaking waves. She breathed deeply, twice.

"Yes," she said, speaking slowly. "I've cut my hair."

"I liked it much better long," he replied instantly. "You realize, of course, that that is the normal masculine preference—all men prefer women with long hair. And in your case especially, Karen, cutting it may have been an important error in judgement. With your particular problem—well, long hair is definitely the intelligent way to go."

He always went unerringly to her weakest spot, she thought despairingly. Her "particular problem" was her crooked old nose, of course. She might have almost forgotten it for a few hours, but trust Edward to remind her. And could it be true that all men liked longer hair? What had Jeff said about it? That it was "nice." But had he actually said that he liked it? *Did* he like it this way? Maybe—

She pulled her wandering thoughts back to the present. What a cruel thing for Edward to say to her. If she had felt any tinge of sympathy for him, of affection left from the life they had shared, he had killed it in that moment.

"It doesn't matter," she said quietly.

"What doesn't matter?"

"Your opinion of my hair length." She felt cold and strange, queerly detached, as though a different person now inhabited her body. "It doesn't matter because you won't be seeing it anymore."

"Now, Karen—"

"Because I'm moving away from Santa Teresa. I don't intend to live in the same town where you are, ever again. Maybe not even in the same state."

"Karen." This time his voice was different. Apparently something in her words had at last carried conviction. Some of his self-assurance had disappeared.

She turned back to face him. He had a stricken look on his face. All at once his favorite jacket looked too big on him.

So he could be hurt, she thought, still in that odd, detached state of mind. Perhaps his emotional bullying was his own way of coping with the world. It could be that he was as flawed and vulnerable as she was.

"You don't mean it," he said, but the protest was weak and unconvincing to both of them.

"You know that I mean every word," she said tonelessly. Some day, far down the years, she might be able to look back on her life with him and feel a trace of the affection she had once had for him. Or at least feel pity. But she couldn't do that now. Not yet. Today there was only this bitter inner coldness, giving her the strength at last to make him know that the break was final.

She could see him now as a tired, unhappy, almost-forty-year-old man. Not the dazzling immortal who had stooped to choose her from the common throng, as she had seen him when she was young and foolish. And not the fearsome ogre of their later years. Just an ordinary man. One that she did not care to see ever again.

"Goodbye, Edward," she said.

He studied her face for what seemed a long time. What he read there, Karen had no idea. The icy coldness inside had made her numb, as though it were an anesthetic. At last his eyes changed, and the air seemed to go out of him as he accepted defeat.

"I'm sorry, Karen," he said.

Her face felt made of stone. Her lips moved only with difficulty. "Goodbye, Edward," she repeated.

His hands started to come up as though he would reach out to her, then they dropped to his sides. He turned away.

Karen watched him briefly as he began to trudge slowly back the way he had come. Then she turned her gaze once more to the fog-shrouded ocean, waiting for the ice to melt inside her, waiting for this emotional numbness to wear off.

The sound of the door closing somewhere in the house penetrated Jeff's sleeping mind. He gradually fought his way through many layers of sleep until he could open his eyes to the gray light that filtered in around the edge of the curtains.

He listened again for the sound that had wakened him, but the house seemed completely still and quiet. The bedside clock showed that it was almost nine. Jeff swore softly as he picked it up and discovered the alarm button was pushed in. He must have turned it off in his sleep. Karen would be here any minute.

He pulled on his clothes, brushed his teeth hastily and ran a comb through his hair before heading for the kitchen and a wake-up cup of coffee to clear the cobwebs from his brain.

The sight of the eggs and tomatoes on the countertop stopped him in his tracks.

"Karen?" he said loudly. Stepping back into the hall, he faced the stairs and raised his voice to call her name again. *"Karen."*

There was no answer. Apparently she had been here and left again. Frowning, he walked quickly into the living room to look through the front windows. Minna's car stood in the driveway, empty. Immediately behind it was a late-model brown Ford that he had never seen before.

"What the hell?" he said under his breath. "What's going on?" The front door slammed behind him as he went out to investigate.

The strange Ford was locked up tight, all four doors. It was covered with road dust, and had California license plates.

Could it belong to Karen's ex-husband? What was his name? Jeff shook his head to clear it. Edward. That was it. The last name still eluded him. Not that it mattered. It wouldn't be him, anyway. It was too soon for him to be here. He couldn't get away until the weekend—had to work or something. Karen certainly wasn't expecting him this morning. Jeff was sure of that. So it must be someone else. On the other hand, he thought bleakly, perhaps this Edward had dropped everything and come on the run.

In that case, where was he? And where was Karen?

Jeff shook his head again, this time in annoyance with himself. If they weren't in the house, there was only one place they were likely to be. He headed for the path down to the beach, covering the ground in long strides. At the top of the slope, he paused to assess the situation. His searching eyes found Karen at once; she was standing at the water's edge some distance up the beach, not moving, apparently looking out at the ocean.

A well-dressed man walked in Jeff's direction, the smooth soles of his leather shoes slipping and sliding on the uneven dry sand above the tide line. As the stranger started up the narrow path, he raised his head, and the sight of Jeff standing above him made him pause momentarily before he doggedly resumed his advance.

Jeff started down to meet him. "What are you doing here?" he asked curtly.

The stranger approached more slowly, his eyes on Jeff. "I suppose you're the new tenant Karen was talking about." He didn't bother to conceal the edge of hostility in his voice.

Jeff instantly detested everything about the other man, from his well-styled fair hair to the leather patches on his jacket. And what kind of a jerk would wear a necktie to the beach, for Pete's sake. This had to be Edward.

When the shorter man reached the point where Jeff blocked the pathway, he stepped onto the wiry grass. "Tell her for me," he said spitefully, talking over his shoulder as he continued climbing the bank, "that I have had it. I'm not going on any more wild-goose chases until she comes to her senses."

Jeff's fists clenched. He hadn't punched anyone since he was in grade school, but a sudden primitive anger made him take a step toward Edward's retreating back. If this little twerp had hurt Karen . . .

He checked his stride at the thought, turned to throw a quick, searching glance at her lonely figure by the water's edge.

Edward wrenched open the car door, slammed it loudly behind him. Shifting the Ford hard into reverse, he backed out of the driveway at a reckless speed.

Alarmed, Jeff could only guess at what had happened between Edward and Karen. It must have been a pretty hostile encounter, judging by the other man's bad-tempered exit. She might be in a very rocky state of mind.

Switching his attention from the fast-disappearing Ford, Jeff ran down the path and across the long strip of sand that separated him from where she stood. Slowing to a walk as he approached her, he said her name in a quiet voice, not wanting her to be startled by his sudden appearance. He reached out to take her gently by the shoulders, and looked down into her tearless face.

Karen felt something inside her come to life again at the touch of his big hands, at the concern she read in his eyes. The strange glacial coldness that gripped her began to slacken.

"Are you all right?" he asked.

"Yes. I'm fine." Her voice felt rusty, as though she hadn't used it for days. And just a few short minutes ago she had been flinging harsh words at poor Edward. Poor Edward? Where had that thought come from? No, she had just escaped from that trap, and she refused to be caught that way again. Edward was gone and no longer any problem of hers. This was her new life. She raised her chin, held up her face for Jeff's inspection. Here she was—crooked nose, short hair and all.

His reaction was all she could have hoped for. The touch of his lips on hers snapped the bonds of ice that had numbed her emotions. She reached up and pulled his head down fiercely. His gentle kiss became a hard, passionate one. His arms circled her, crushed her to him.

She held him tightly as cold turned to warmth, to heat, to passion. His body burned against her. Sudden, scorching desire swept through every fiber of her being.

Surprise and shock impelled her to break the embrace, to push him away—even though her body clamored to continue, to pursue this all-encompassing feeling to its ultimate destination.

Her own audacity left her breathless. Her lack of confidence had dictated all her previous dealings with men. She was always careful not to demand more than her partner offered to give, and had certainly never offered more than that partner had shown himself eager to receive. But then, she had never felt quite like this before.

She drew a shaky breath, tried to smile, to smooth over what had just happened. She forced lightness into her voice. "I—I guess I'm not quite so calm as I thought I was. It must be a reaction to—to—" *To you, to your kiss, to your strong and vital body pressed against mine!*

But there was no way she could tell him any of that. She hesitated, then continued, " . . . a reaction to the relief of finally making a clean break with Edward."

"It's final, is it?" There were frown lines between his eyebrows as he looked down at her.

She didn't want him to frown ever again. She wanted to kiss away each small line, to use her lips, her body, to make him happy forever.

She closed her eyes against this strange giddy abandon. Jeff's supporting arms encircled her.

"Are you all right?" His voice was sharp with concern.

She allowed herself the luxury of relaxing against him, feeling his lean strength once more. "The break is definitely final this time. And I'm fine," she reassured him. "Finer than I've been in years."

He made a noncommittal sound deep in his throat, as though still not quite convinced.

That was all right, she thought dreamily, in time he would see that she was right. And they had time. Hours and days stretched out in front of them. Time to be together, time for her to show him the new Karen. New both inside and out. His arm tightened around her, and she sighed with pleasure.

"I think I see someone coming this way," he said.

She could tell from the tone of his voice that that someone was definitely not Edward. "Who is it?" she murmured, not bothering to turn her head.

"I don't know. Maybe the old fellow who was beachcombing along here the other day."

The other day. The day she had pulled away and run like a frightened deer at the thought that other eyes might see them embracing. It was hard to believe she had actually done anything so silly. As though it mattered what other people thought or said. The important thing—the only important thing—was to be right here, in Jeff's arms.

Jeff turned her gently in the direction of the house. With his arm still around her shoulders, he moved them slowly back the way they had come. Karen walked beside him contentedly. Privacy would be nice, too. As long as they were together. In front of her, the day seemed to be unfolding like a flower, like a sunrise, full of promise.

Once inside the kitchen again, Karen took off her jacket and stretched expansively.

"You sit down," Jeff said. "I'll fix us some breakfast."

Lovely as it was to be coddled and cared for, right now she felt as healthy and happy as she had ever been in her whole life. "I don't need to sit down. And I thought you said that you couldn't cook."

"I can scramble eggs." Jeff picked up the carton.

Karen took hold of his wrist with one hand and deftly removed the carton from his grasp with the other. "This morning we are having omelets, bacon, the works. I brought all the makings."

He turned his hand over to catch hold of hers. She gave him a mock-severe look. "Don't distract the chef when she's creating a masterpiece." She freed herself with a quick, flashing smile. "You can be vice-president in charge of toast."

Jeff felt reluctant to let her have her way, but he sat down with a brief shake of his head. It was not in his nature to sit back and let someone else take charge. Not when he felt he was needed. And he wasn't sure that these sudden high spirits of hers would last. Still, he had to admit that her smile brightened the old kitchen even more than the sunshine that was beginning to glow through the thinning fog outside.

He waited until she served the food and took her place opposite him before he asked the question that was on his mind. "What makes you so sure Edward won't be bothering you anymore?"

Karen paused to think out her answer. "He knows now that I mean what I say. And I told him I'm leaving Santa Teresa."

"Do you think that's what convinced him?"

She had to force herself to remember exactly what she had said to Edward. The actual words were already becoming hazy in her mind; what she recalled most vividly were the ugly emotions, that cold numbness she hoped never to feel again. "I'm not certain just what did it. Something made him realize—something changed him. I'm sure he won't try to get in touch with me when I go back."

"Go back?" Jeff said, surprised.

"I'll have to quit my job properly, give them two weeks notice or however much time they need to replace me. Not that that should be so hard. They're already getting along without me."

"What kind of a job is it?" he asked.

"Just general office work. For a little venetian-blind business that needed someone part-time to type and answer the phone a couple of years ago. And you know how it is in an office—I gradually did more and more, learned new things. Until after a while I was working full-time."

Jeff looked at her curiously.

"What is it?" she asked.

"I'm just trying to picture you out job hunting, the way you were before. When did you start all this?"

"You mean, was I married? And did Edward approve? No, he hated the idea. But I needed something to do. He didn't want children when we were first married, and later on, I didn't think it would be a good idea, either. Not with our marriage being so shaky. But I didn't actually start by reading the want ads. A friend told me the job was available, and I scraped up my courage and went to inquire. Lucky for me I got it. I wouldn't have left Edward without being able to support myself."

"And what will you do now?" he asked.

That was a big question.

Playing for time, Karen slowly cleared away the plates and refilled their coffee mugs. The emotional mood swings she had undergone this morning had leveled out. Now she was feeling clear eyed and calm. And quietly cheerful. The future was indeed cloudy and unreadable. But for the first time she could remember, she could look ahead without a knot of anxiety forming under her breastbone—and without wanting to escape into the old fantasy of solving all her problems by having plastic surgery some day in the far-off future.

"I'll get another job," she said finally, making her voice brisk and positive. She thought that they had better get off this subject; it brought to mind too many other unspoken questions. Once she moved from Santa Teresa, where was she going to live? Here in Nelsmith with Minna? In Portland, where jobs were more plentiful? Or—just maybe—in the San Francisco area?

The final answer depended on the developing relationship between Jeff and herself. And that needed time. It was too soon for either of them to put their feelings into words. But if the outside world would leave them alone for a while, alone together, perhaps some of those questions would answer themselves.

She said, "I suppose you're anxious to get back to what you were doing before Tim came—finishing up your program's heart transplant."

Jeff smiled a little sheepishly. "I suppose so," he agreed without enthusiasm. "But these last few days seem to have knocked it completely out of my head. It'll take me a while to get back at it."

He settled back in his chair. They sat quietly, not speaking, just being together. Karen glowed inwardly that he should be content to idle the time away in her company. Silence seemed to stretch between them, a quiet that somehow managed to hum with unspoken messages, a tingling awareness....

The telephone rang, and Karen jumped. She glanced at the clock, then turned an apologetic face toward Jeff. "That's probably Minna. She needs her car back by two-thirty to show a house," she said, reaching for the receiver.

"Hi, Karen," Tim said in answer to her hello. "Is the head honcho available?"

"Tim!" She stared at the instrument in her hand in disbelief. "Where are you? Still in Portland?"

"Heck, no. I'm hard at work in the office, like every other powerhouse business manager on this lovely Saturday afternoon."

"But you can't be! Your plane just left a little while ago."

"I flew out of Portland early this morning. Before the crack of dawn. You didn't expect me to do something frivolous like going home to say hi to my goldfish, did you? Not me. I went from the San Francisco airport to the office and straight to work. And straight into another mess that only His Honchoness can handle."

"Just a minute, Tim. I'll put him on."

Jeff leaned toward her and held out his hand.

She gave him the receiver with a little exasperated headshake and a raised-eyebrow look that invited him to share in her annoyance.

Jeff didn't seem to notice. His sharpened attention was focused on the telephone. "Tim?" he said tensely. "What is it? What's happened now?"

Karen felt uncomfortable sitting at the table listening to their conversation as though she were eavesdropping. But the only alternative—leaving the room—could be interpreted as a petty or bad-tempered action. At least, it would seem that way to her, because she actually felt surprisingly aggravated at Tim's untimely interruption.

Not that Jeff would notice whether she eavesdropped or not, she realized after a few uncomfortable minutes. He listened to a long explanation from the other end of the line with a concentration so complete that she suspected the solid old kitchen had temporarily ceased to exist for him—along with everything in it. Including herself. From the look on his face, only Tim's disembodied voice coming through the telephone receiver was real at the moment.

At last he spoke. "Read me that letter," he instructed Tim.

Karen had no luck deciphering the nature of the problem from the rest of the conversation. Jeff spoke in monosyllables or short, elliptical phrases that conveyed little meaning to her.

"Yes, all right," he said, finally. "I'll do that. Yes, as soon as possible. Yes. Okay. Goodbye." He put the receiver back on its cradle but continued to sit lost in thought, as though unaware of his surroundings.

"Trouble?" asked Karen sympathetically. As soon as she spoke, she wished she could call the word back. Of course it was trouble. Tim didn't call long-distance on the weekend to let him know everything was rosy. "I mean, is it something important?"

He didn't answer for a moment. Then he blinked and seemed to remember that she was there. "There's a problem, yes. And it's important. Our biggest corporate account is having trouble with the customized software we installed for them a month ago. I can handle it—only it's going to take me some time."

She didn't like the way he said that. It gave her the uneasy feeling that something was about to interfere with the very special dinner she had planned for tonight. If Jeff was unwilling to stop working, perhaps she should postpone it until another night? Or—and this thought was even worse—were they in for another visit from Tim?

She recalled what Tim had told her about Jeff keeping the reins of company management tightly in his own hands. "This happens quite often, doesn't it?" she said.

"What do you mean?"

"Problems and questions keep coming up, and you're the only one who can handle them."

He nodded. "That's true."

"Does it have to be like that?" She wanted to give him an impassioned argument on the subject of delegating responsibility. It was folly to run a business of any size as such a one-man operation. But she held back the words. He had heard all of that from Tim already. And she had no right to tell him how to run his business. Or his life.

She said, "I mean, shouldn't you have a vice-president or something. To take care of times like this. To make decisions when you're not there."

He shook his head, frowning. "I never go away and stay away like I've done this time. I'm always there. I should be there now. I'm the only one who can handle this situation. I have to go back."

Chapter Nine

Stunned, Karen stared at him. This was worse, much worse, than any canceled dinner or unwelcome visitor. Surely he didn't mean what he'd just said! He couldn't be leaving! What about his work, his program that wasn't finished? Was he going to pack up and leave it undone? *What about us?* a small anguished voice inside her cried.

Through stiff lips, she said, "When will you—?" She stopped, afraid that her voice would break and betray her feelings.

The faraway look had returned to his eyes. It was as though he had already left her in spirit. His body might be so close that she could reach across the table and touch him, but his mind, and heart, were no longer with her. He apparently hadn't even heard her few choked words, since he didn't answer her question. Karen couldn't ask it again, because she couldn't speak. She could barely breathe.

At last her words seemed to penetrate his consciousness. He turned to her, but still with the same distracted air. "When will I leave?" he said. "Today. Right now. As soon as I can throw my things in the car."

She wanted to pound the table and scream at him, to tell him to *look* at her, tell him to tear himself away from business long enough to think about what he was leaving. But of course she couldn't do any such thing.

Choosing her words carefully, she said, "Wouldn't it be better to wait and go in the morning? You could get a good night's sleep and make an early start."

"But I just had a good night's sleep. And a great meal." He patted her hand. "I'll be fine."

Jeff stood briskly, almost as though he couldn't wait to be on his way. "I'll load the computer stuff in the trunk of the Volvo," he said, speaking half to himself, half to her. "And throw the rest of my things in the back seat."

As soon as he left the kitchen, left her sitting there alone, Karen's defenses went down. A tidal wave of misery engulfed her. She pressed her hands flat against her midriff in a futile effort to ease the hurt. It felt as though someone had driven a stake through her heart.

How could he be so unfeeling! Black despair rolled over her, dragged her down into its depths, stripped away all there was of brightness and joy in the world, robbed her of confidence and strength. Weak and unworthy, unwanted, unloved—that was all she'd ever be.

She let herself be swept along by the tides of bitterness and anger that surged through her. How could he be so cruel! Making her believe in herself. What a poor deluded fool she'd been, parading around with an *imaginary dog*, no less. He had made her believe in passionate kisses and happy endings. And love. And now he was snatching it all away!

"Don't cry! Don't cry! Don't cry!" she told herself in a desperate, rapid whisper. Eyes burning, throat tight, she fought an internal battle, willing herself to hold back the tears. She managed a victory, but it was only a temporary one. Once he was gone, she would lay her head on her arms and cry her heart out. Let her heart break in private, once she was alone.

He has no idea how badly he hurt you. The clear, cold thought pierced the roiling darkness in her mind. She shook her head. That was no comfort. How could he walk away from her like this, with no apologies, no regrets— almost eagerly?

Karen got up from her chair and began to pace the kitchen floor with quick, staccato movements, her arms crossed tightly under her breasts, holding herself together.

She felt brittle, cold, as though her self-control was a fragile thing liable to shatter at any moment. But, for the moment, it enabled her to assume a weird sort of calm. Her words came out cool and emotionless.

"I'll go in the other room and see if I can help him pack," she said aloud, experimenting with this new voice. Feeling as hard as glass, as fragile as the thinnest crystal, she went to help him pack his things to leave her.

Driving fast and competently down the coast road, Jeff decided to swing inland and pick up the freeway on the other side of the Coast Range. This road was good, but it necessarily had to follow all of the curves and dips of the shoreline, and it was only two lanes wide. The morning's fog had evaporated to a slight milkiness in the blue of the sky, but it would probably thicken again by evening. And that would slow him to a crawl and require his complete concentration to navigate safely. In the long run, the freeway would get him there faster.

Already he had thought of a handful of ways that the shipping company employees might have mishandled their data input. Those would be comparatively easy to isolate and safeguard against. But if there were bugs in the program itself, that would be a whole new ball game.

As he was in the midst of mentally designing a complex new testing procedure, a picture of Karen's face slid into his mind. A picture of Karen waving goodbye outside the old beach house as he drove away after kissing her briefly and promising to call when he reached home.

Home, he thought wryly. He certainly didn't expect to see much of his own apartment until this mess was straightened out. He'd catch some sleep on the plane to Houston as soon as Tim finished briefing him on the full extent of the problem. Somewhere along the way he'd squeeze in a minute to telephone her.

She had taken his sudden departure extremely well, he thought. Somehow he had expected a few tears, even re-criminations.

But she had been wonderful about the whole thing. Helped him pack and then waved him on his way. No resentment, no clinging, no questions.

And after that last embrace on the beach, she might very well have considered herself entitled to lengthy explanations.

That wasn't the first surprise Karen had given him in the past few days. Each time he thought he knew what to expect from her, the unexpected happened.

That stylish Karen, suddenly so beautiful, with green eyes a man could drown in, where had she sprung from? He could scarcely connect the gentle, timid little creature who had needed his help with the confident young woman who handled Tim Broderick so offhandedly. The woman who had sent that jackass Edward on his way, looking as though a mule had kicked him in the head.

It had seemed to him that he had found the first Karen once more when her arms had embraced him so hungrily on the beach afterward. But those same arms had waved him on his way without a protest.

Frowning, he shook his head grimly. He liked things to be logical, to make sense. Karen Grenville baffled him more than—than any question of what had gone wrong with the Houston Shipping Company's expensive new computer system. At least he had a fighting chance to solve *that* problem. Providing he could put her out of his mind long enough to concentrate on business.

When the Volvo disappeared from sight, Karen turned toward the house, wiping away her tears with her hands, trying to stem their sudden flow. She wanted nothing more in the world than to let go, to let all her disappointment and grief pour out. But there was no time to cry. Not quite yet. She had to hold herself together long enough to take the car back to Minna.

Karen washed her face vigorously in cold water. Looking in the mirror, she saw the same plain, unhappy reflection that had looked back at her for as long as she could remember. If she let her hair grow long again, she would be the same as before. No, she could never be quite the same again. For she had lost the conviction that had sustained her all these years. She no longer believed that having her nose straightened would solve her problems. She had already given her appearance her best shot—and what was the result? Jeff was gone. So quickly, so easily—without a second thought—he was gone.

She stuffed the towel back on the rack and walked listlessly out to the car.

As she drove, she wondered if he would ever call her as he had said he would. She was afraid to pin her hopes on a careless, last-minute promise. Not when he could leave so quickly, so easily, as though all that mattered to him was the excitement and challenge of that other life.

She parked in front of the real-estate office in Nel-smith, took the keys in with her and dropped them on Minna's desk. Her aunt gave her a long appraising look, but remained mercifully silent about her bedraggled appearance.

"Is Mr. Forrester coming back?" Minna asked.

Karen shrugged, not even curious to know how the news had spread so fast.

"He stopped and left me the extra house key," Minna said. "He said that the place is all yours now, if you want it. I offered to refund the money he had coming, but he wouldn't wait. I'll send him a check in the mail."

All Karen wanted was to be left alone. "I'd like to stay at the old house—if that's all right with you," she said.

Minna started to speak, then apparently thought better of it. After a thoughtful pause, she said, "As soon as I'm free, I'll run you back out there, then, if that's what you want." She looked at her watch. "I've got a client coming in just a few minutes."

Karen shook her head. The sensible thing would be for her to go to Minna's place, pack her things and wait to be driven back to the beach house. But she didn't feel able to be sensible anymore. She had to get away from polite conversation and other people's eyes.

"I'd just as soon walk." She looked down at her old clothes and smiled without mirth. "As you can see, I'm not wearing high heels today."

"Here comes my client." Minna sounded distracted. "Walk, then. Or wait at my house. Do whatever you want. I'll bring your things out later."

"If it's not a bother," Karen said dully. She didn't care if she never saw those clothes again.

"Just a minute," Minna called after her as she started out the door. "Do you have anything to eat out there?"

She suddenly recalled the steaks in the refrigerator, the ones she had so joyfully purchased for herself and Jeff. The remembrance was a blow. Had it only been this morning when the world was so shining and perfect? Right now the very thought of food sickened her.

"There's more than enough," she answered her aunt. "Don't worry about me."

Karen trudged the three miles with her head down, eyes on the shoulder of the road ahead of her plodding feet. Her body felt as if it wanted to curve inward, to shield her inner self from any more hurt.

The sun burned through the remnants of last night's fog, but a brisk little breeze from the north made her turn up the collar of her jacket. The weather was completely out of sync with her emotions. The clouds ought to be heavy and dark, the ocean booming, whitecapped rollers smashing against the shore and trees thrashing their limbs against the sky.

Karen put one foot in front of the other, half remembering landmarks from all the times she'd walked this stretch of road as a teenager, ten years ago. She recalled this viewpoint, a turnout where tourists could stop their cars, with its low stone fence that made a good resting spot. There was the blackberry patch on the other side of the highway. And, up ahead, the crossroads store.

She plodded on, slowly but steadily, determined not to cry. Not yet. She was ten years too old to walk along a public highway with tears running down her face.

No, tears would have to wait a little longer, another mile, a half a mile, until she started down the sandy road that led to the beach house. At last she reached it and was finally able to turn her back on the highway. Now let them come, she thought recklessly. The hot pressure that had burned behind her eyelids every step of the way found its release.

The house came into view, empty windows staring at her from its weathered gray facade.

"Damn!" she said uncharacteristically as a new thought struck her. Minna would be along any time now, once she got rid of her latest client, bringing Karen's things. Karen couldn't present herself as a sobbing bundle of misery in front of her aunt. These feelings were too private for that.

She wiped her face and sniffled back the torrent of tears that were still waiting to be shed. She started to turn the key in the lock . . . and discovered in herself an enormous reluctance to go inside the house.

There were too many memories lurking in those rooms, waiting to overwhelm her fragile self-control. Jeff at work. Jeff asleep and herself yearning over him so tenderly just a few hours ago, when she was so happy. The amethyst dress in the upstairs closet, the food in the refrigerator—everything was waiting to stab her in the heart with what might have been.

Forcing herself to unlock the door, she hurried straight to the kitchen, left a "Gone to the beach" note for Minna and fled out the back door and down the sandy path.

Karen tramped along the firm wet sand, heading northward until the rocky headland reared up before her,

the waves breaking in white foam where sheer cliffs met
the water. As she turned and began retracing her steps,
fatigue overwhelmed her.

An ancient driftwood log, tossed high above the tide-
mark by some long-ago winter storm, offered a resting
place. She plodded through the loose sand and sank down
on it wearily. She rested her face in her hands and closed
her eyes. All of the thoughts she had been trying to hold
at bay leaped instantly to her mind.

A faint doggy whine preceded the touch of a cold, wet
nose on the back of her hand. For a moment her heart
stopped. Her eyes flew open. A nondescript brown mon-
grel was studying her earnestly.

"Oh," she said, her voice shaky. "Who are you?" She
stroked the shaggy coat, found a half-hidden collar and
identification tag. "Hello, Rusty."

The dog bobbed his head at the sound of his name, then
leaned against her leg as she continued to pet him. Drawing comfort from his furry warmth, she found her voice
steadying as she went on talking.

"You don't happen to have a tall friend called Otto, do
you, boy? A silky fellow with a long aristocratic nose?"

Rusty closed his eyes and turned his head so she could
scratch below his other ear.

"No, I guess not," she said. Karen felt exhausted, but
all the walking that had worn her out also seemed to have
burned off a little of the emotional turmoil that had con-
sumed her. Now a precarious, eye-of-the-storm calm had
settled over her.

She got to her feet with an effort. Minna might be
waiting at the house, worrying about her. The small
brown dog ambled companionably at her heels as she re-
traced her steps. Minna's car stood in the driveway. Karen

braced herself for a lecture as she opened the kitchen door.

The warm smell of fresh coffee floated out to mingle with the sharp fresh tang of ocean breeze. Karen put out her foot to bar Rusty from coming inside. "He followed me up from the beach," she said.

Minna turned from the cupboard with two cups in her hand. "Oh, yes, he lives across the highway."

The dog pricked his ears and sat up hopefully in the doorway.

"You know you're not supposed to beg from the neighbors," Minna told him, her voice severe. "The vet put you on a diet months ago." She hesitated. "Well, maybe just half a cookie." A plate on the table held fresh oatmeal-raisin cookies. She broke one in two and brought it over to the expectant animal. "Now go home, Rusty."

She shut the door firmly and turned to Karen. "I'm starved. I brought some stuff to make myself a sandwich. Do you want one?"

Karen shook her head. "No, thanks. I don't feel much like eating." She took off her jacket and hung it on the hook beside the door.

Minna didn't argue. She set two cups of coffee on the table and pushed the cookie plate in Karen's direction, then went briskly about fixing avocado and bacon sandwiches on white bread.

The scalding-hot liquid warmed Karen's inside. The heaviness in her chest loosened as she sat and watched her aunt. Presently her hand went out of its own accord and took the other half of Rusty's cookie from the plate.

Just as she was feeling alone and unloved, she thought, Minna had remembered her favorite cookies and stopped at the bakery to bring them to her.

"I brought your clothes," Minna said. "I hung your suit in the closet up in your old room, so you'll have it to wear when Edward gets here."

Karen sat up straighter. "Edward's already been here, Minna."

Her aunt's busy hands stilled. "What? Where is he?"

"I'm not sure where he is now," Karen said. "I told him to check into a motel and get some sleep before he started back. But he was pretty upset when he left here. I expect he drove for a while before he calmed down enough to feel like sleeping."

"*Edward* was upset? And you never even mentioned he'd been here!" Minna looked at Karen as though she had grown two heads.

This morning seemed like a very long time ago to Karen. "I guess I forgot," she said.

"You forgot," her aunt repeated softly, shaking her head in wonder. "Well, when did all this happen? What did he say?"

"He got here early—before breakfast. He said—" she stopped to think "—he said all the usual things." For a moment she had difficulty remembering his specific words. "He told me I used bad judgment, cutting my hair. That I should keep it long, because of my 'particular problem.'"

Minna frowned. "What did he mean by that?"

"You know." Karen touched the bridge of her nose. "He always told me that long hair was best. To hide behind." She paused again. "No, this time he didn't actually say that part about hiding. But that's what he meant."

"Edward did *that*?" Minna compressed her lips tightly. She said no more, but the butter knife in her hand clattered onto the countertop with unnecessary force.

That was the sound of Edward sliding off the pedestal where Minna had always placed him, thought Karen.

Minna cut the sandwiches crosswise and arranged the triangular wedges on two plates, one of which she placed firmly in front of Karen. "What are you going to do now?" she asked.

Karen didn't know how to answer. The future seemed as impenetrable as the densest fog bank. "Stay here, I guess."

"By yourself?" Minna's voice was questioning, but not unkind.

Karen looked down at her untouched food. "Jeff said he would call me here."

"Oh." Minna ate neatly, efficiently, as she did everything else. "When?"

"He didn't say."

They were both silent for a moment.

"No matter how fast he drives, he won't reach San Francisco until well after midnight," Minna said. "You shouldn't expect to hear from him until tomorrow morning at the earliest."

Slightly cheered by this practical assessment of the situation, Karen absentmindedly began to eat the sandwich on her plate. Of course, she told herself, she should have been pinning her hopes on that promised telephone call rather than letting disappointment tear her apart as she had. Minna was most likely right; she couldn't expect to hear from Jeff until tomorrow morning. After breakfast, even.

But if he called while she was asleep, she'd never hear the telephone ringing here in the kitchen. What if she missed him! Misery stood poised at her elbow, ready to engulf her again. Karen wasn't about to let it happen.

She'd sleep on the living room couch. She'd surely hear the telephone from there.

Nearing the end of his six-hundred-mile drive, Jeff stopped at a roadside telephone and woke Tim Broderick from a sound sleep.

"Yes, I know it's two-thirty in the morning," he told his yawning subordinate. "I'm fifty miles up the road, and I'll get to the office in an hour or so. I want you to meet me there. Bring lots of black coffee."

By the time Tim—still yawning—arrived at the office with coffee and doughnuts—Jeff was there and already deep into the original specifications for the shipping company installation.

"Go call the airport and get me on the earliest flight to Houston," he told Tim without raising his head from the pile of papers in front of him. "And then call the shipping company. Tell them to have somebody who's familiar with the problem meet me at the airport and take me straight to their main office."

"You do know that today is Sunday?" Tim asked mildly.

"All the better. I can run diagnostic tests without having to work around their normal operations."

Tim came back to report that Jeff was booked on the sunrise flight to Houston, leaving at six-thirty-four, and that a shipping company vice-president would be on hand to meet him when he landed.

"Good." Jeff looked at his watch. "Pull the rest of these files for me, will you? And keep an eye on the clock to make sure I leave in plenty of time. I need to eat a meal at the airport. Then I'll try to get some sleep on the plane."

But once on the plane, sleep didn't come easily. Thoughts of Karen crowded in on him, and he found himself unable to put them aside. Too bad he hadn't had a chance to telephone her before takeoff, but he'd just made the plane without a minute to spare. There hadn't even been time to eat, so he'd have to stay awake for the airline breakfast. He promised himself that he would call her at the first opportunity. The first minute he could arrange to be alone...

Jeff opened his eyes again as the plane nosed down to land at the Houston airport. He sat up and ran his fingers through his hair as he mentally reviewed his plan of attack for finding the reason behind the shipping company's problem. A picture of Karen slid into his mind, disrupting his calculations.

As he stepped into the terminal, he looked around for the nearest telephone. A well-dressed but harrassed-looking man intercepted him before he had gone ten steps.

"Are you Forrester?" he demanded. At Jeff's nod, he said, "Thank heaven you're finally here. Are we going to be able to resume business in the morning?"

"We have to isolate the problem first." As Jeff began to explain the necessary steps, the man laid an insistent hand on his arm and drew him toward the exit, where a chauffered car was waiting.

The man, who proved to be the shipping company vice-president responsible for computer operations, stayed stubbornly at Jeff's elbow for the rest of the day. He became an annoyance, a distraction. As Jeff immersed himself deeper and deeper in the problem, he dealt with the vice-president's presence by forcing himself to narrow the focus of his attention until everything else disappeared from his consciousness. He ate the food they brought in for him, but minutes later would have been unable to remember what it was. Day turned into night and became morning again.

A bleary-eyed and unshaven Jeff finally put his finger on the culprit. "Here it is," he told the equally rumpled vice-president. "An operator error that triggered a whole landslide of other errors."

The other man looked at his watch. "It's three in the morning. Monday morning. Am I going to be open for business at nine o'clock?"

"I'm afraid not. It's going to take a lot of work to straighten this out. I'll call my office manager and get him to send a team of technicians on the first plane, now that I know what has to be done."

Replacing the receiver after giving Tim his instructions, Jeff remembered that he hadn't yet called Karen. He was so exhausted that it took him a minute to work out the time difference between Houston and the West Coast. It was the middle of the night there, and he was too groggy to think of what to say to her, anyway. He lay back on the leather couch in the vice-president's private office. Sleep overwhelmed him.

Karen had stayed in the house all day Sunday, waiting for Jeff's promised telephone call. She had tried to keep herself too busy to think, dusting and cleaning, but as the time went by, she found herself staring out of the kitchen window, not seeing the sand or the ocean but reliving all the hours of yesterday. Hours that she wished she could get out of her mind.

All of her fine new self-confidence had deserted her the moment Jeff had said that he was leaving. As though it truly had been only skin-deep, she thought.

Because of things he said and did, she had been inspired to change her life. Now that he was gone, she might as well admit that she would always be plain, timid, shy little Karen. Would always need someone with more authority to tell her how to act. Edward was right—

Wait a minute, she thought.

Edward definitely was *not* right. She didn't need to get carried away with self-pity here. She had done some things that were praiseworthy before Jeff ever came into her life. Some things that were even pretty brave, as she looked back on them. Getting a job, for instance. And keeping it in the face of Edward's disapproval.

And getting her divorce! That was the hardest decision she had ever made. It cost her a great deal of agonizing, but she had made up her mind. And stuck to it.

All that happened long before she knew Jeff Forrester existed, Karen told herself. A few days ago she had dealt with Minna as an equal. And after that she'd had no difficulty in talking to Tim. And all by herself she had made Edward accept that the break between them was final. There *was* strength in her. She could stand straight and hold up her head, even if she had to do it alone. Without Jeff.

But that wouldn't happen. He said he would call. And he would. Any minute now.

All during the morning she told herself that he was probably sleeping after his long drive. Through the long afternoon she clung to the thought that he was working and too busy to call.

But when evening's black shadows closed in around the house, she acknowledged to herself how worried she was. He might have had an accident along the road. Surely if he had arrived safely, by now he would have picked up the telephone to tell her so.

Now that she had talked herself out of yesterday's despair, she refused to let herself slide back into useless tears again. So she paced the floor dry-eyed, picturing the white Volvo crumpled in some lonely ravine, with Jeff trapped inside....

Fear overcame any last shred of pride she had left. She called Minna—very briefly, so he wouldn't get a busy signal if he was trying to call—and asked for his home telephone number. She *had* to find out if he was safe. But arrangements to rent the beach house had been made through his office, so Minna had only a business number for him. That meant that Karen had to wait another twelve hours before she could hope to find someone at the switchboard in his office.

She slept on the couch again, dozing fitfully and coming awake with a start a dozen times through the endless night.

It was one minute to eight when she got through on the telephone to Forrester Software. "I'm sorry," the receptionist said brightly. "Mr. Forrester hasn't come in this morning."

Chapter Ten

For a black, heart-wrenching moment, Karen couldn't breathe, couldn't speak. Finally, through dry lips, she managed to ask for Tim Broderick.

"Jeff's in Houston," Tim told her in reply to the question she could barely bring herself to ask.

"Houston?"

"You know, where all the trouble is. I talked to him earlier this morning. He called to have me put a couple of the technical staff on a plane and hustle them out there. He thinks he's tracked down the problem."

"Oh." That was all she was able to say.

"Do you want me to give him a message the next time he calls in?" Tim asked cheerfully.

"No. No, thanks, Tim. I—it wasn't important." Karen said goodbye and hung up quickly.

She'd made a fine fool of herself, hadn't she! Pacing the floor, picturing him lying broken and bleeding in a ditch somewhere, and all the time he was perfectly fine. In

Houston. And he could reach a telephone to call his office when he wanted to. But not to call *her*.

A sudden wave of anger swept through Karen, catching her by surprise. As always, her first reaction was to deny it, force it down.

No, she thought, I've got a right to be mad, to be good and mad! I've waited and worried and lost sleep over this. He could very well have called, and he just didn't do it.

"Damn!" she said aloud, shattering the placid stillness of the kitchen. *"Damn, damn, damn, damn, damn!"*

She slapped her hand down hard on the wooden table, making her palm sting. She hit the table once more, with a clenched fist this time, feeling a grim sort of pleasure in the noise it made, in giving her emotion free rein. Now she could see why people raised their voices and slammed things around. Letting it all out did bring a certain satisfaction. A great deal more than she'd ever experienced by holding her feelings in and curling up into a tight little bundle of misery whenever things went wrong.

She'd have to give Jeff credit for one more thing. He'd taught her to appreciate the full pleasure of losing her temper!

Karen walked the floor until her anger simmered down a little, but enough fire remained in her veins to make her look around and see her present situation from a new perspective. This house all at once seemed like a backwater, a detour off the main road of her life. She shouldn't be idling here, wasting time. She didn't even have her own means of transportation. She ought to be getting after the insurance company in Santa Teresa to replace her wrecked car.

The time had come to leave this place of memories, both bitter and sweet. It was surprising how a dose of anger could turn out to be a great backbone stiffener, she thought ruefully. All at once she couldn't wait to get away.

She called Minna. "I'm packing my things. I'm going back to Santa Teresa."

"You are?" Minna's voice showed her surprise. "Right now? Today?"

"Yes, today. On the next bus."

"What's the rush? I'll come out and we'll talk it over."

"I've made up my mind," said Karen.

"I'll be there in fifteen minutes." Minna hung up.

Karen dragged her small suitcase out of the closet and threw it on the upstairs bed. As she packed, she braced herself for the forthcoming argument with Minna. She was going. That was definite. There was no room for discussion.

Something told her that if she wavered now, she might weaken entirely. Her sweet, reasonable side—her *doormat* side—even now whispered to her not to go away, that Jeff would surely call soon.

Soon just wasn't good enough, countered her new, willful self. How long was she supposed to fold her hands and wait for him to think of her? Until tomorrow? Next week? *Christmas?*

She finished packing her clothes and went downstairs to clean out the refrigerator. A once-superb steak was the first item into the black garbage bag.

Minna came in through the kitchen door. "I've closed the office for the day."

Karen mutely continued dumping perishables into the big plastic sack.

"I was thinking—" Minna hesitated. "I wondered—if you've really made up your mind to go—would you like some company on your trip? We could drive my car."

Karen stared at her. "You mean—as far as Portland?"

"No." Minna sounded tentative, unsure of herself. "To Santa Teresa."

"Oh." Karen took a moment to absorb the idea. "Really? Would you do that? I mean—*could* you? What about your office?" she asked.

"There's no point in having your own business if you can't take some time off when you really want to. None of the men I know would hesitate to close up shop to go fishing. Or play golf."

That was very true, thought Karen. If a man really wanted to do something, such as take a vacation—or make a telephone call—he did it. Especially if he owned the company.

"A little southern California sunshine would be a nice change," Minna went on. "And it would be an opportunity for us to get acquainted all over again. I feel like you've turned into someone I hardly know."

Karen nodded at that. She *had* changed. And so had everyone around her—Edward, Minna— A shiver ran through her. Perhaps Jeff had changed, too.

"Can we leave today?" she said.

Minna thought for a minute, then nodded. "Why not?" she said.

Two young men from Forrester Software's technical staff arrived at the Houston Shipping Company's main office shortly after noon on Monday. Jeff briefed them on his findings.

"This is where these people went wrong," he said, putting his finger on the problem. "This is the snarl they got themselves into. And this is how we're going to repair the damage. I want you two to get started unraveling the mess. And after you do that, we'll have to devise some safeguards so they don't wind up in this situation again.

If you need me in the next few hours," he said, "I'll be using the couch in the vice-president's office to catch up on lost sleep."

Jeff felt like a diver just breaking the surface after a long, deep submersion. The weight of an ocean seemed to be sliding off his back. In a little over forty-eight hours he had broken the back of a potentially serious problem. There would be a few more days of cleanup work, but the worst was over. Even his extreme tiredness couldn't blunt the sweet satisfaction of a difficult job well done. Jeff closed the door of the vice-president's office and reached for the telephone, eager to tell Karen the whole story.

After eight rings he broke the connection and dialed again. Still no answer. He frowned. Somehow he hadn't expected her to be outside. Perhaps she was down on the beach.

He rubbed his eyes. They felt as if they were full of sand, and his lids were still heavy. Oh well, he thought, as fatigue claimed him, I'll have to try again in a couple of hours. I can give Karen the good news then.

In a hotel room later that evening, he made half a dozen attempts to reach her and met with the same lack of success. Jeff tried Minna's number. No answer there, either.

He supposed it was possible that the two of them were out somewhere together, unlikely though that sounded. And it didn't seem a bit like Karen, not to be there when she was expecting this call.

The next day when he went back to the job at hand, it was with diminished enthusiasm. His concentration wavered, and Karen's face kept coming between him and his calculations. He would see the full curve of her lips and the way she nibbled at the lower one whenever she was uncertain, the radiance of her smile when she insisted on cooking breakfast the day before yesterday.... No, come to think of it, it was longer ago than that. Saturday morning. And this was Tuesday. He'd lost track of a day in there, somewhere....

Still, a day more or less shouldn't make any difference. Karen certainly had no plans to go anywhere. None that she'd mentioned to him, at least. And she surely would have told him if she'd intended to leave. On the other hand, he'd left Nelsmith in a hell of a hurry....

At midnight Jeff gave up trying to work. He left the job in the hands of the technicians and went back to the hotel. But once he got there, the last, late unanswered rings of her telephone left him baffled and uneasy, and his sleep was fitful and disturbed.

He flew back to San Francisco in the morning. And Karen still didn't answer her telephone. At the office he decided to try the number at half-hour intervals while he went ahead and cleared up his regular paperwork. But each thirty minutes dragged on like an eternity. The ordinary day-to-day details that were piled up on his desk began to seem like an irritating waste of time.

"Don't we have anyone qualified to deal with some of this minor stuff?" he demanded of Tim Broderick in the middle of the afternoon.

Tim looked at him quizzically.

"Okay, okay," said Jeff. "I know what I said before. Now I'm saying that I don't want to fool with it any longer."

"I'm happy to hear it." Tim looked at the mess of papers covering Jeff's desk. "Just hand over everything you want to get rid of, and I'll work out an assignment roster to take care of it."

Jeff culled his In basket ruthlessly as Tim waited, and finished up by impulsively adding a couple of his pet projects to the pile. "These are interesting, but they're minor stuff. I can't handle everything myself. And don't bother saying 'I told you so.' Just be sure to include some kind of reporting system so we'll know who's doing what.''

"Right." Tim seized the stack of files and started for the door as though eager to get away before Jeff could change his mind and take them back. "It'll take me a little time to sketch out a table of organization. When that's ready, we can sit down and hash out the details. Okay?''

Jeff nodded assent. More than thirty minutes had gone by since his last attempt to reach Karen. He put his hand on the telephone. "Sure, Tim. Talk to you later. I'm going to call Karen."

Tim paused in the doorway. "By the way, she called here earlier in the week."

Jeff stared at him. "She did? She called *you*? When? What did she say?"

"It was first thing Monday morning, just as the office opened. She asked for you, but you weren't here, so she talked to me. She wanted to know where you were, and I told her you'd gone to Houston."

"What else did she say?"

Tim shifted his load of papers from one arm to the other. "Nothing."

"Come on, she must have said *something*."

Tim frowned. "As near as I can remember, she said 'Oh.' And 'goodbye.' And hung up."

Jeff dialed her number again and listened mechanically to nearly a dozen rings while his mind tried to make sense of Tim's conversation with Karen. There was no logic to it. Why would Karen call here? What had happened? If it was important enough for her to try to reach him, then why didn't she leave a message? At least she could have left word where he could get in touch with her.

Baffled, he pushed aside the remaining papers on his desk. If Karen wasn't at the beach house, where in the world could she be?

The answer to that was anywhere in the world. Mexico, Canada, wherever. She had no ties. She could go wherever she pleased.

That line of thinking was no help.

On the other hand, he knew of one other specific location where Karen still *did* had ties. Her apartment and job were down in Santa Teresa. He couldn't imagine why she might return so suddenly, but at least he had one more place to look.

He picked up the phone and asked for Directory Assistance for the city of Santa Teresa. They gave him her listed number.

But no one answered there, either.

All he could think of was that it didn't make any sense. The Karen he knew wouldn't go off somewhere and not let him know. At least, not the sweet, gentle Karen who had first touched his heart. There was no denying that a changed Karen had come back from Portland.

Everything had been so perfect between them until she had spent those few days in the city. In fact, she had changed noticeably as soon as they had got there. The minute they'd hit Portland, something mysterious had happened to Karen.

Jeff pushed his chair away from the desk. Maybe he could think better on his feet. He was accustomed to problems he could solve with his intellect, accustomed to analyzing, getting down to basics, bringing order out of chaos. Taking charge.

But there was nothing he could get hold of here. He shook his head. This emotional stuff didn't play by logical rules. It absolutely didn't make sense that Karen wasn't available at the other end of the telephone line. And it was even more incomprehensible that he should be pacing the floor of his office because of it.

And that wasn't all. The papers remaining on his desk had undergone a change as mysterious as anything else that had happened. He had already unloaded all the trivial daily stuff by giving it to Tim to take care of, so the remainder was the very heart of the business—the meaty, fascinating, important problems that challenged him, that made life fulfilling. All the things that made him willing—eager—to work twelve hours a day, every day of the week.

Right now he felt he'd gladly drop the whole lot of them off a bridge somewhere. Then he could go to Karen. If he only know where she was! Compared to her, business decisions shrank into insignificance. At this moment he could turn his back on all this stuff in front of him, just close the door and walk away.

Sure he could, Jeff told himself sarcastically. He could walk away. And in a couple of days he'd be yanked back by another frantic phone call. Like a yo-yo on a string.

Damn it, he didn't own this business—the business owned *him*!

The thought jolted him. He dropped into his chair and stared at his desktop with set jaw. Did he really believe that? Had he buried himself so deep in work that he could never dig himself out even if he wanted to? If that was the case, he had a bigger problem than he had realized. One that he had to face up to right now.

Every day he was called on to make decisions; this would be the most important one of his life.

Jeff sat immobile as the moments ticked by. Presently he roused himself to press the intercom button to speak to his secretary.

"Get me Tim Broderick. Right away. And tell him to bring that table of organization with him."

Two days later, in the middle of the afternoon, Jeff dialed the beach house, Minna's office and then the apartment in Santa Teresa for what seemed the hundredth time. Finally the receiver in the apartment was lifted, and Karen's voice said, "Hello?"

"Karen?" he said, hardly able to believe that his luck had finally changed.

"Jeff!"

The quick pleasure in her voice gave him a little jolt in the area of his heart. "Where have you been?" he demanded, surprise and relief making the words almost harsh.

Karen paused. She had fully intended to be distant and aloof whenever Jeff finally got around to contacting her. On the long drive down from Nelsmith, she had brooded over his parting words. He *would* call, she told herself. Sooner or later. Someday, somehow, she would hear from him again. And when that time came, she would be cool, reserved, not wear her heart on her sleeve. She couldn't forget those agonizing hours of waiting, worrying about his safety.

But when she heard his voice, all her stern resolve had melted in the uprush of warmth and happiness that swept over her. Even his rather peremptory tone failed to crush the singing in her heart.

"Where have I been?" she said cheerfully. "I've been out shopping for a new car."

"I mean where have you been for all these days and days I've been trying to get hold of you? And why are you back in Santa Teresa?"

A variety of retorts flashed through Karen's mind. Flippant: everybody has to be somewhere. Aggrieved: how long did you expect me to sit by the telephone waiting for you to get around to call? Hostile: I don't hear from you for nearly a week, and now you want to know where *I've* been?

No, she wouldn't start a quarrel over the telephone. It was just too wonderful to hear from him at last. On the other hand, perhaps she shouldn't go back to her old doormat self, either.

"Oh," she said, coolly innocent, "have you been trying to telephone me?"

"Have I been trying—" Words seemed to fail him. "What do you think I've been doing all this time! I told you I'd call, didn't I?"

Karen bit back a swift, barbed retort. Instead of answering, she simply kept quiet.

The long silence after his words seemed to make Jeff realize just what he had said. "I did mean to call you, but I had a lot of problems getting to a phone. And once I got to Houston, I was all tied up. It was always either too early to call you or too late."

"I was worried about you," she said finally.

"Worried?" He sounded completely nonplussed.

"You started out on a long drive through the night. When I didn't hear anything from you, I was afraid you might have had an accident."

"You shouldn't even think things like that." He spoke quickly, dismissively. Karen didn't answer. After a pause he said, almost shyly, "You really did worry about me?"

Karen thought of that terrible sleepless night, of the heart-stopping moment on Monday morning when she learned he hadn't arrived at his office. She forgot about being cool and unemotional.

"Of course I did!" All her pent-up anger burst forth. "You had to drive hundreds of miles in the dark and the fog, and you said that you'd call but you never did! And then Tim said you were *fine*—you'd just gone on to *Houston*—" She stopped abruptly, shocked at her own aggressiveness.

He didn't answer at once. Her heart beat erratically as she waited. What had she done! She never intended to attack him. But all the hurt and anger inside her had forced its way out.

"I didn't realize," he said at last. "I'm sorry."

The relief of tension left her weak. Karen found that she'd been holding her breath, fearful of his reaction. She was still so new at standing up for herself that she expected the sky to fall at every confrontation.

Jeff was still talking.

She made herself pay attention to his words.

"... so it was the middle of the night when I got to the office," he was saying. "And my plane left so early I couldn't call without waking you up." He went on to explain about not having a free moment until after midnight because of the problems he'd run into, trying to figure out where the shipping company had gone wrong. After a while his side of the conversation evolved into a highly technical dissertation on computer technology.

Karen listened to the words blissfully, not trying to follow his explanation but smiling fondly at the enthusiasm in his voice.

Jeff broke off in midsentence. "You don't want to hear all this," he said.

"Of course I do." A loyal answer, if not a strictly truthful one.

"No," he said. "It's time to talk about you. How long will you have to be in Santa Teresa? Are you going back to your job?"

"No, they already have someone who can take my place. I just have to get another car and dispose of some of the things in my apartment. Then I can leave Santa Teresa."

"And where will you go?"

That was an important question. Karen tried to answer it matter-of-factly. "Back to Nelsmith, to start with."

"And then—?"

"Minna thinks I might be able to sell real estate," she said. "She wants me to get my license and work with her."

"You don't want to do that." He spoke quickly, positively.

Karen stiffened a little. "What do you mean?"

"Well—you and Minna would be together all the time. She's not the easiest person to get along with, you know."

"If it didn't work out, I suppose I could always try something else."

"I guess so." He sounded unconvinced. His voice changed, became more positive, as he said, "What are you doing this weekend?"

Karen gripped the receiver more tightly. He almost sounded like someone about to ask a girl for a date. "I— I haven't made any definite plans," she said.

"Maybe I could drive down to Santa Teresa and see you...." He let the suggestion hang in the air.

Karen hesitated. It was sensational that he should even entertain the idea of making a round trip of nearly a thousand miles to be with her. On the other hand, there was something that he didn't know. "Minna is staying here with me," she told him.

"Minna? In Santa Teresa? Why? What's she doing there?"

"Taking a little vacation and helping me to get things straightened around. We drove down from Nelsmith in her car."

"I didn't think Minna was the type to take off suddenly like that." Karen could almost hear the frown in his voice.

"It *was* rather surprising. A spur-of-the-moment decision," she said.

"What did she do—just lock the door and walk away?" Jeff persisted.

"That's right. Minna said there was no point in owning the business if that meant she could never get away from it," Karen added unthinkingly.

"I see," he said. Just those two words, nothing more.

Karen felt a rush of contrition, of alarm. Did he suppose she'd said that on purpose, throwing it up to him? Was he hurt? Offended? Oh, dear...

After an awkward little hiatus in the conversation, Jeff went on. "Maybe Minna has a point there." Then, his voice more businesslike, he said, "Look, Karen, I've got a meeting with Tim in a few minutes."

Karen could almost see him withdrawing his attention from her. "Yes, of course," she said, trying to keep her voice cool and emotionless to cover her hurt. "I understand. You're busy."

"No, that's not what I mean," he replied swiftly, apparently sensing the change in her tone. "I just mean that this isn't the best time for us to talk. I'll call you this evening." He paused, then added belatedly, "If you're going to be home."

"I'll be here." Karen's voice was soft. "I'll be waiting.

Though Jeff called that evening—and regularly every evening after that—he did not after all drive down from San Francisco to see Karen. Minna's presence made a reasonable excuse for not making the trip, but there was another, stronger reason he didn't come to Santa Teresa. By mutual agreement, it was decided that the next time they met it would be in familiar surroundings, in the beach house at Nelsmith.

Karen cleared up her business in Santa Teresa in a week and a half, taking time for a little judicious shopping and even a trip up to Disneyland with Minna. It was a fine liberating day when she turned in her apartment key and slid into her new blue Honda to follow Minna onto the highway.

She was not unhappy that Jeff hadn't come to Santa Teresa. Hearing his voice on the telephone every evening was a poor substitute for actually having him with her in person, but Karen felt that their next meeting should be a private one—just the two of them, together at last.

As she hung her clothes in the closet in the beach house, she made plans for that long-anticipated meeting. She hung the amethyst dress—as yet unworn because Jeff had to be the first one to see her in it—in a special niche of its own.

The day came at last. Jeff was on his way. By sundown he would arrive.

Karen had everything ready by midafternoon. The steaks waited in the refrigerator, and candles were on the table. There remained the driftwood logs to be laid in the fireplace, and then she could change out of her old shirt and jeans. The next time Jeff saw her, she would be wearing amethyst silk that would shimmer in the candlelight.

She was on her knees on the brick hearth when the front door was flung open and Jeff's tall figure blocked out the light.

"I'm here!" he announced, spreading his arms wide. "I left early!"

Karen caught her breath. Joy flooded her body at the sight of him. He came toward her, and she stood up into the welcoming circle of his arms. All her imagining was a pale thing compared to the reality of his touch. Her skin tingled. Her blood sang. As he held her close, love overwhelmed her, blotted out everything else. This was the only thing that mattered—not a silk dress still hanging in the closet, not expensive makeup waiting unused on her dresser. . . .

"Karen!" He drew back to look at her, his dark eyes shining. "I can hardly believe it! Here you are—exactly as I've been picturing you every mile along the way."

"Not like this!" She laughed a little shakily and ran a finger along the bridge of her nose, the old nervous gesture she thought she had left behind her. "I've probably even got a smudge on my nose."

He kissed the tip of her nose lightly. "An adorable smudge." With a gusty sight of contentment, he pulled her close. "You're perfect just the way you are."

Karen held him tightly, her hands flat against the muscles of his back, her head on his shoulder and her eyes wide with dismay. Could it be—was it possible—that he had come back hoping to find the *old* Karen? The little Country Mouse of their first few days together? It was true that those had been long, sweet hours, when they first learned to know and trust each other. He had worked, and she had drifted through the house like an unsubstantial wraith, each one seemingly comforted by the other's presence, happier knowing the other was there.

Was that what had drawn him to her—her unobtrusiveness? But Jeff was the one who had told her to hold up her head, to face up to the world. He couldn't possibly prefer the original, unimproved Karen.

Or could he?

He had shown none of his present enthusiasm for her more stylish, more confident self when she returned from those few days in Portland. Then he had been very quick—almost eager—to leave her and return to work. And now he seemed so very pleased to find her like this—all drab and dusty as she was.

She couldn't think straight while he held her, his cheek against her hair, the warmth of his lean body finding an echo in her own innermost depths. She stirred in his arms, pushed herself away.

His embrace tightened for a second. Then he let her go.

"You can put your suitcase in your old room," she said brightly. Too brightly. "It's all ready for you. And—and perhaps you'd like a shower before dinner."

"That sounds fine." He looked a little puzzled and slightly deflated.

Karen automatically touched her forefinger to the slight irregularity of her nose, then snatched her hand down when she realized what she was doing. She forced a brief smile. "I—I have to change, too," she said. And fled upstairs.

She huddled in a chair by her bedroom window. The grayness of the sea and sky outside reflected her own feelings. Her whole attention turned inward, searching the core of her being. If Jeff really wanted a humdrum little homebody, could she be that kind of person again? She certainly had had plenty of practice. It felt as though she'd lived the past twenty years of her life in a small, windowless room, afraid to step outside and face the world, using the excuse of her imperfect face as a reason not to try.

Somehow she had at last found the key to open the door that imprisoned her.... And then Jeff came along to give her the incentive to step out into the full glare of the sunlight. Now she could feel that she was truly a part of the world that she had avoided for so long. Even though she did still need a few props occasionally, such as fashionable clothes or an imaginary dog.

But what if Jeff wasn't interested in a more confident, outgoing woman? His ideal could easily be someone who would love him and keep his house and shield him from any demands on his time that would interfere with his dedication to his work.

Was it too late to turn back the clock? She could be that kind of a wife. Surely she could.

But she had spent four years trying to be the kind of wife that Edward wanted—and that had been a disaster for both of them.

After her little taste of freedom, could she retreat into that windowless room again?

Chapter Eleven

Karen stood in front of the open closet door for what seemed an eternity. Plain old blue jeans and no frills—that was the way he thought of her. She didn't really need to change at all; she could just wash her face and walk down the stairs. Walk back into Jeff's waiting arms, the one place in the world she longed to be. Back into the tight confining little niche where he seemed to feel she belonged.

The temptation was overwhelming. She closed her eyes. If only he would love her, she could surely turn herself into whatever it was he wanted her to be. And he *did* want her; she almost believed that now. Jeff hadn't made all this effort, come all this distance, on some careless whim. And if she believed that, how could she ignore the things he'd said downstairs? How could she go ahead and flaunt her new self in his face.

She couldn't take a chance on losing him, not for all the bright-colored silk in all of the stores in the world. She could live a lifetime without another expensive dress. That would be easy. A lifetime without Jeff was unthinkable. The decision was clear-cut. Or was it?

The truth was that fancy clothes were far from the important issue at stake. They were only the outward sign of the inner change in herself. The change Jeff had helped to bring about—and which he now seemed willing to repudiate.

Oh, why was she still standing here? She knew what she wanted. More than anything else, she wanted Jeff's love and to be allowed to love him in return. The way to reach that goal seemed plain: walk down the stairs and show him the kind of woman he was looking for. If she no longer quite fit the description, he never needed to know.

Would that be fair to him? To either of them? In five years, or ten, would she find it necessary to fling open another door and make a second escape in order to be able to breathe again?

Tears slid down her cheeks. She longed so terribly for him to love her. All she had to do was cheat a little bit, pretend to be something she wasn't. Be a little bit dishonest. She was so very afraid that to be honest with Jeff meant she would lose him.

Karen walked down the stairs as tensely as a French aristocrat going to the guillotine. As she reached the landing, she saw that Jeff had finished building the fire. The flames leaped and crackled in the shadowy living room, the sound drowning out the faint whisper of silk against her skin.

Jeff stood up as she entered the room. Her breath caught in her throat as he turned on the standing lamp beside the couch. He had changed into corduroy slacks and a pullover sweater. Expensive, good-looking clothes.

Casual clothes. What a mismatched pair they made! And it was all her own fault. She smoothed the amethyst silk across her hip with a nervous hand. Her steps faltered, stopped.

Jeff came forward, looking at her intently, unsmiling. He took her hand and drew her into the light. His serious expression struck coldness to her heart.

He studied her for what seemed an eternity, from various angles, up and down, even turning her halfway around and then back again with the hand that still held hers.

He shook his head, half frowning. "You're beautiful."

She took a step back and made a quick gesture of denial. "No, I'm not." Her free hand rose instinctively toward her face before she stopped it in midair.

"Yes, you really are beautiful." He sounded to her like a scientist who had made an unexpected discovery, but she couldn't tell from his voice whether he was pleased or disappointed with what he had found. "And that's a beautiful dress."

Karen bit her lip as she looked down at the clinging silk. The crucial question was not whether he liked the dress itself, but how he liked her in it. She had to know the answer. "Do—do you really like to see me dressed like this?"

"Of course," he said. The intensity of his scrutiny never slackened. "Who wouldn't?"

She was not satisfied. Had there been some reservation in his voice, or did she just imagine it? "You're sure?"

"Absolutely. You look wonderful, Karen. Perfect."

Before she could stop herself, she blurted out the one thing uppermost in her mind. "You didn't seem to feel that way the other day—when Tim was here—and I was wearing my new suit—"

"I didn't?" He gave her a puzzled frown.

Karen stared back at him, appalled at her own reck-lessness. It was as though some stranger had spoken through her lips, forcing the issue that she had agonized over but couldn't bring herself to mention. Her first instinct was to retreat, explain, smooth things over some-how. But she caught back the words, made herself return his gaze in stubborn silence.

He looked away into the brightly colored flames play-ing over the burning driftwood. "Maybe there's some-thing in what you say. I guess at the time I didn't...exactly...*appreciate* the change in you," he said at last.

Her worst fears were suddenly confirmed. Karen felt the breath go out of her lungs. Strength and confidence drained out of her. She had believed that she was pre-pared for that answer. Now she realized that she had still been clinging to hope. And that hope had just been snatched away....

He shook his head. "I guess until then I'd been taking it for granted that you and I were the same kind of peo-ple," Jeff went on musingly, as though talking to him-self. "I know I'm not a very sociable type. Not like Tim. I've always been too busy for playing." He freed her hand and put his arm around her shoulders, drawing her closer. "No, that's not quite right. I'm trying to be honest here. The truth is that I arranged my life to keep it that way— so full of work that no one could expect me to make time for the really hard things. Like having fun. Or a family." He paused. "Or falling in love."

His last word seemed to echo in the silence that fol-lowed. Phantom bells chimed...*love*...*love*...*love*...

Karen stood rigid, scarcely breathing, afraid to move or speak lest she shatter the moment.

The quiet acceptance in his voice tore at her heart. She desperately wanted to comfort him, make him happy, tell him that she would fill his life with all the things he'd been missing. But she had learned these past weeks that that was not something that another person could do for you. Someone else could reach out, but you had to reach back. Meet them halfway. You had to be willing to take chances, go through the fears and the difficulties. . . .

Still silent, she put her hand on his arm, feeling the rough texture of his sweater against her palm and the warmth of his body.

"Then you came back from Portland," Jeff said, "and you were suddenly all poised and confident. And beautiful. Different." He broke off to glance at her, then turned toward the fire again. "And I thought—" He stopped again. "No, looking back, I can see that I wasn't doing much coherent thinking just then. I guess that I just *felt* that I didn't really know you anymore. That I couldn't go where you were going. That I had nothing to offer—"

"Oh, Jeff," she murmured, burrowing into his arms, holding him tightly. "That isn't true. And it doesn't matter." If he loved her, they would make it work. Somehow. "None of that matters."

"Oh, yes, it does," he said positively. Then he seemed to hesitate. "Let's sit down, shall we?" Suiting his actions to his words, he sat at one end of the couch and drew her down after him.

Inside the comforting circle of his arms, her head resting on his shoulder, Karen felt blissfully secure. Regardless of what he was going to say, there had to be some way to make it work for the two of them.

"It matters a lot," he said. "I've made a tremendous discovery. There actually are more important things than work." He gave a short, self-deprecating laugh. "I guess I know how Columbus felt when he found America. I don't exactly know where I'm at or what to do about it, but I can see I've stumbled onto something big."

"Jeff—" She breathed his name. His arms around her tightened slightly as he went on talking.

"I decided that one thing I can do is try out some of Tim's organizational ideas. This past couple of weeks we've been setting up a system to give me some free time. Fixing things so I can take my hands off the controls now and then without the whole company going into a nose-dive."

Sheer surprise propelled her upright. Her eyes searched his face. "*Really?* You did that?"

He nodded, his expression lightening, the ghost of a grin lurking around his mouth. "Yes, really. If I get shipwrecked on a deserted island, the business will stagger along without me. For a while, anyway. Long enough to let me take care of some of the more important things. Like this."

He pulled her against him once again. His lips met hers in a long, hard kiss—a triumphant, walls-come-tumbling-down, bursting-fireworks, toe-curler of a kiss.

When Karen came up for air, she felt lightheaded with happiness. Giddy, gasping for breath, she laughed. "You—you did all that? Just so we won't be interrupted this time? So the telephone won't ring—?"

"It had better *not* ring," he said with mock fierceness. "If it does, heads will roll!"

"Wonderful!" She pressed her cheek against his. "So they won't snatch you away this time."

"This time or any other time," he said emphatically. Then, with obvious reluctance, he added, "Well, not with any luck at all. If a real catastrophe comes along, then I'd have to go back. But whatever happens, they're going to at least try to handle it themselves. After all, that's what they'd do if—"

"I know." She whispered. "That what they'd do if you were shipwrecked on an island. Do you think—is there any chance you might be cast away any time soon?"

"You never can tell." Jeff looked immensely pleased with himself. "But now I'm prepared—just in case you'd like to take a cruise on our honeymoon."

Karen's whole world seemed to change around her, leaving her speechless, giddy, her blood fizzing in her veins like uncorked champagne.

"What do you think?" he asked.

She tried to sit up again, but he held her tightly against him. "What do I think about what?" she managed to ask faintly.

"About a cruise, of course." He looked down at her straight-faced, but mischief danced in his eyes.

"Oh, that." She tried to put on a thoughtful frown, but there was too much happiness in her for anything but smiles. "I thought you were talking about honeymoons."

"That, too."

"I think—I think there must be a few details to take care of before—before..." Her voice trailed away questioningly.

"I know," he said more soberly. "This big, important one that I haven't mentioned yet. Karen, will you marry me?"

"Oh, yes." She put her hand up to touch his face. "As long as you're sure—"

"I was never more sure of anything in my life," he said with feeling. "And let's make it soon. This falling in love is hard on the nerves. I guess I'm ready for a nice long sea voyage."

"I seem to remember," she said thoughtfully, "that you once mentioned a cruise as being your idea of nothing to do."

He gave her a determinedly nonchalant look. "As long as we're together, I'm fairly sure that we can find something to pass the time. Like this." He kissed her again.

She smiled up at him. "For twenty-four hours a day?" she asked.

"Why not?" His eyes were shining, and Karen knew that her own must look the same.

In this new happiness, this new ease with each other, Karen discovered in herself a little imp of playfulness that she had never allowed to surface before.

"Why not, indeed," she said mock-severely. "And come home with paralyzed lips, no doubt. Maybe—if we really try—we can think of something else to keep you amused."

"What did you have in mind?" he said, smiling and waggling his eyebrows suggestively.

"Oh," she said airily, "you could work on your suntan, I suppose." The idea of Jeff lying in a deck chair doing absolutely nothing was the most unlikely thing she could imagine.

"Who, me?" he said, matching her mood. "I never worked on a tan in my life."

"Scratch that suggestion, then. How would you like to go dancing?"

"Well, now," he said slowly. "Maybe. I've seen people dance. It doesn't look too hard."

She stared at him. The corner of his mouth quirked upward in spite of his attempts to stay poker-faced. She gave him a loving little shake. "Don't tell me—you're really a wonderful dancer! Another Fred Astaire."

He let the grin break through. "I haven't been on a dance floor for years. But there was a time when I wasn't too shabby out there. The right partner might bring out the best in me."

She settled back with her head on his shoulder. "If all else failed, we could always eat something. Don't they serve a dozen meals a day?"

"Talking of eating—"

His joking tone hadn't changed, but Karen was suddenly aware of the lateness of the hour. The blackness of night had taken over the world outside the windows.

"Oh, you must be starved," she said quickly.

"Well," he admitted, "not quite. But I wouldn't say no to one of your famous omelets."

"We'll have something better than that." She moved to get to her feet, but he held her back for one more kiss. And then another...

"Let me go get my apron on," she whispered finally. "At this rate we'll both starve."

As she got to her feet, it seemed as though everything around her had taken on a new luster; all the colors were brighter, deeper, stronger. Even the tired old kitchen seemed rich and strange. Her acute awareness of his nearness quite overwhelmed the mundane reality of cooking dinner; each casual touch became a meal-threatening distraction. He handed her a pot holder when it was time to turn the meat under the broiler, and the steaks almost burned as she smiled up into his eyes.

Tearing her gaze away, she hurriedly reached for the tongs. There was a scratching at the kitchen door and a short commanding bark from outside.

Her hands were full. "Will you get a dog biscuit out of the cupboard?" Karen called. "The neighbor's dog has gotten in the habit of stopping by for a handout every evening."

Jeff found the box. "How many?"

"Just one. Rusty's on a diet. Just hand it to him, and he'll go home."

When the steaks were out of danger again and the door had closed on the departing Rusty, Karen paused with the tongs still in her hand.

"Do you think we could have a dog someday?" she asked.

"I don't see why not." Jeff slid his arms around her from behind, bent his head to rest his cheek against her hair. "I don't know how well a dog would fit in my apartment. But then I guess we'll be needing a house, anyway, won't we? With a big yard and everything?"

Karen nodded, the picture in her mind too wonderful for words—herself, Jeff, kids, dogs, green grass and picket fences. . . .

She forced her attention back to the here and now, carefully checked the steaks once more. "Could we have an Afghan?"

"An Afghan? Oh, you mean the dog. Is that what you'd like?"

Karen slipped out of his embrace and turned to face him. "Don't you think I'd look kind of elegant with a big Afghan hound on a leash?"

"You'd look elegant even with a junkyard mutt." He reached for her hand, apparently no more willing than she was to be out of touching distance. "That dress alone ought to be going around the world on the *Queen Elizabeth II*."

Another mention of a cruise. She found it heart-catchingly endearing, this eagerness of his to show the change in himself by voluntarily embracing what was once the most boring existence he could imagine. She had no desire to put him to such a test.

"If you don't mind too much," she said, "I'd just as soon we kept our feet on dry land for a while."

A brief shadow that might have been relief passed over his face, but it was gone too quickly for Karen to be sure.

"Whatever makes you happy," he said.

A candlelit dinner in front of the fireplace, with Jeff sitting across the table from her, meant that Karen didn't taste a single bite of what she managed to eat. Their conversation ran along in queer little fits and starts. One minute they would be making solemn plans for the future, and then they'd look into each other's eyes and forget what they were saying.

In the middle of one of these silences, she said suddenly, "What would you think of Otto for a name?"

He was slow to answer. "Otto?" Then, dubiously, "You like the name Otto?"

"Don't you?"

"Well..." He pushed away his empty plate and cleared his throat. "Otto Forrester?" he said unenthusiastically.

"I know it's an unusual name for a dog, but—"

He threw back his head with a shout of laughter. "*For the dog!* That's different! You had me worried for a moment there." He stood up and reached for her hand.

As she rose to meet him, everything around her suddenly crystallized into an instant of perfection. A shimmering breathless moment of pure love, pure trust, pure happiness. A moment to remember for a lifetime—for the lifetime they would live together.

*   *   *   *   *

COMING NEXT MONTH

**#760 ONLY THE NANNY KNOWS FOR SURE—
Phyllis Halldorson**
A Diamond Jubilee Book!
Nanny Heather Carmichael knew her proper place in the Sheffield
household—and it certainly wasn't on the arm of Max, youngest Sheffield
sibling. But Max—and a Revolutionary spirit—knew otherwise. Now to
convince Heather...

#761 PICTURES OF EMILY—Theresa Weir
Sophisticated Sonny Maxwell had lived life in the fast lane, but St. Genevieve
Island was far from the high life. Could Emily Christian teach him to enjoy the
simpler pleasures in life—like family, love and marriage?

#762 CRANE'S MOUNTAIN—Adeline McElfresh
When Glen Moran arrived on Laura Crane's doorstep bearing bittersweet news,
Laura soon hoped the roving reporter would uncover enough romantic evidence
to spend a lifetime on Crane's Mountain!

#763 JUST IN TIME FOR CHRISTMAS—Moyra Tarling
When Drew Sheridan returned with his son to patch up a family feud, Vienna
Forrester decided to help. But the Sheridan men were so...so...*stubborn*!
Could they ever become a family in time for Christmas?

#764 SMART STUFF—Karen Leabo
Although genius Camille Gordon needed Baylor Pierce's help in tracing some
missing files, she hadn't expected his constant surveillance. By working
together, could the book-smart physicist and the street-smart detective close the
file on love?

#765 HOME FOR THE HOLIDAYS—Doreen Roberts
Sarah Wainwright didn't want anyone to be alone for the holidays, especially
not Officer Reid Colton. He tried to convince the determined beauty to drop
her persistent pursuit but he soon realized that he *was* lonely, and always would
be—without Sarah.

AVAILABLE THIS MONTH:

The tradition continues this month as Silhouette presents its fifth annual Christmas collection

SILHOUETTE

Christmas

STORIES
1990

The romance of Christmas sparkles in four enchanting stories written by some of your favorite Silhouette authors:

Ann Major * SANTA'S SPECIAL MIRACLE
Rita Rainville * LIGHTS OUT!
Lindsay McKenna * ALWAYS AND FOREVER
Kathleen Creighton * THE MYSTERIOUS GIFT

Spend the holidays with Silhouette and discover the special magic of falling in love in this heartwarming Christmas collection.

ARE YOU A ROMANCE READER WITH OPINIONS?

Openings are currently available for participation in the 1990-1991 Romance Reader Panel. We are looking for new participants from all regions of the country and from all age ranges.

If selected, you will be polled once a month by mail to comment on new books you have recently purchased, and may occasionally be asked for more in-depth comments. Individual responses will remain confidential and all postage will be prepaid.

Regular purchasers of one favorite series, as well as those who sample a variety of lines each month, are needed, so fill out and return this application today for more detailed information.

1. Please indicate the romance series you purchase from regularly at retail outlets.

Harlequin	Silhouette	
1. ☐ Romance	6. ☐ Romance	10. ☐ Bantam Loveswept
2. ☐ Presents	7. ☐ Special Edition	11. ☐ Other _____
3. ☐ American Romance	8. ☐ Intimate Moments	
4. ☐ Temptation	9. ☐ Desire	
5. ☐ Superromance		

2. Number of romance paperbacks you purchase new in an average month:

12.1 ☐ 1 to 4   .2 ☐ 5 to 10   .3 ☐ 11 to 15   .4 ☐ 16+

3. Do you currently buy romance series through direct mail?   13.1 ☐ yes   .2 ☐ no

If yes, please indicate series: _____

(14,15)   (16,17)

4. Date of birth: _____ / _____ / _____
                 (Month) (Day) (Year)
                  18,19   20,21   22,23

5. Please print:
   Name: _____
   Address: _____
   City: _____ State: _____ Zip: _____
   Telephone No. (optional): (_____) _____

MAIL TO: Attention: Romance Reader Panel
         Consumer Opinion Center
         P.O. Box 1395
         Buffalo, NY 14240-9961   ☐☐☐☐☐☐☐☐☐☐☐☐

                                    Office Use Only   SRDK

Take 4 bestselling love stories FREE

Plus get a FREE surprise gift!

PASSPORT TO ROMANCE
SWEEPSTAKES RULES

1. **HOW TO ENTER:** To enter, you must be the age of majority and complete the official entry form, or print your name, address, telephone number and age on a plain piece of paper and mail to: Passport to Romance, P.O. Box 9056, Buffalo, NY 14269-9056. No mechanically reproduced entries accepted.

2. All entries must be received by the CONTEST CLOSING DATE, DECEMBER 31, 1990 TO BE ELIGIBLE.

3. **THE PRIZES:** There will be ten (10) Grand Prizes awarded, each consisting of a choice of a trip for two people from the following list:
    i)   London, England (approximate retail value $5,050 U.S.)
    ii)   England, Wales and Scotland (approximate retail value $6,400 U.S.)
    iii) Carribean Cruise (approximate retail value $7,300 U.S.)
    iv)   Hawaii (approximate retail value $9,550 U.S.)
    v)   Greek Island Cruise in the Mediterranean (approximate retail value $12,250 U.S.)
    vi)   France (approximate retail value $7,300 U.S.)

4. Any winner may choose to receive any trip or a cash alternative prize of $5,000.00 U.S. in lieu of the trip.

5. **GENERAL RULES:** Odds of winning depend on number of entries received.

6. A random draw will be made by Nielsen Promotion Services, an independent judging organization, on January 29, 1991, in Buffalo, NY, at 11:30 a.m. from all eligible entries received on or before the Contest Closing Date.

7. Any Canadian entrants who are selected must correctly answer a time-limited, mathematical skill-testing question in order to win.

8. Full contest rules may be obtained by sending a stamped, self-addressed envelope to: "Passport to Romance Rules Request", P.O. Box 9998, Saint John, New Brunswick, Canada E2L 4N4.

9. Quebec residents may submit any litigation respecting the conduct and awarding of a prize in this contest to the Régie des loteries et courses du Québec.

10. Payment of taxes other than air and hotel taxes is the sole responsibility of the winner.

11. Void where prohibited by law

COUPON BOOKLET OFFER TERMS

To receive your Free travel-savings coupon booklets, complete the mail-in Offer Certificate on the preceeding page, including the necessary number of proofs-of-purchase, and mail to: Passport to Romance, P.O. Box 9057, Buffalo, NY 14269-9057 The coupon booklets include savings on travel-related products such as car rentals, hotels, cruises, flowers and restaurants. Some restrictions apply. The offer is available in the United States and Canada. Requests must be postmarked by January 25, 1991. Only proofs-of-purchase from specially marked "Passport to Romance" Harlequin® or Silhouette® books will be accepted. The offer certificate must accompany your request and may not be reproduced in any manner. Offer void where prohibited or restricted by law. LIMIT FOUR COUPON BOOKLETS PER NAME, FAMILY, GROUP, ORGANIZATION OR ADDRESS. Please allow up to 8 weeks after receipt of order for shipment. Enter quickly as quantities are limited. Unfulfilled mail-in offer requests will receive free Harlequin® or Silhouette® books (not previously available in retail stores), in quantities equal to the number of proofs-of-purchase required for Levels One to Four, as applicable.

OFFICIAL SWEEPSTAKES
ENTRY FORM

Complete and return this Entry Form immediately—the more Entry Forms you submit, the better your chances of winning!
• Entry Forms must be received by **December 31, 1990**
• A random draw will take place on **January 29, 1991**
• Trip must be taken by **December 31, 1991**

3-SR-3-SW

YES, I want to win a PASSPORT TO ROMANCE vacation for two! I understand the prize includes round-trip air fare, accommodation and a daily spending allowance.

Name_____

Address_____

City_____ State_____ Zip_____

Telephone Number_____ Age_____

Return entries to: **PASSPORT TO ROMANCE**, P.O. Box 9056, Buffalo, NY 14269-9056

© 1990 Harlequin Enterprises Limited

COUPON BOOKLET/OFFER CERTIFICATE

Item	LEVEL ONE Booklet 1	LEVEL TWO Booklet 1 & 2	LEVEL THREE Booklet 1, 2 & 3	LEVEL FOUR Booklet 1, 2, 3 & 4
Booklet 1 = $100+	$100+	$100+	$100+	$100+
Booklet 2 = $200+		$200+	$200+	$200+
Booklet 3 = $300+			$300+	$300+
Booklet 4 = $400+	_____	_____	_____	$400+
Approximate Total Value of Savings	$100+	$300+	$600+	$1,000+
# of Proofs of Purchase Required	4	6	12	18
Check One	_____	_____	_____	_____

Name_____

Address_____

City_____ State_____ Zip_____

Return Offer Certificates to: **PASSPORT TO ROMANCE**, P.O. Box 9057, Buffalo, NY 14269-9057

Requests must be postmarked by **January 25, 1991**

- ✂- - - -

 **ONE PROOF OF PURCHASE**   3-SR-3

To collect your free coupon booklet you must include the necessary number of proofs-of-purchase with a properly completed Offer Certificate

© 1990 Harlequin Enterprises Limited

See previous page for details